Alice's Diary

The Memoirs of a Cat

Chilton Designs Publishers, Publishing House, Trinity Place,
Barnstaple, Devon EX32 9HG

First published in the United Kingdom
by Chilton Designs in 1989

Reprinted 1992, 1995, 1996, 1997, 1998, 1999, 2001,
2002 (twice), 2003, 2006, 2007 (twice)

Set by Bath Press Intergraphics, Avon

Printed and bound in Great Britain by Antony Rowe Ltd.,
Chippenham, Wiltshire

A catalogue record for this book is available from
the British Library

ISBN 0 9503527 1 3

Alice's Diary

The Memoirs of a Cat

*Dedicated to
all cat lovers with
grateful thanks from a
cat
who loves humans*

About the author

Alice is a 6 year old mixed tabby. She lives in Devon and shares her home with her half sister Thomasina and two humans. This is her first book. Her hobbies include sleeping, eating and sitting in the sun.

January 1st

Thomasina and I got into terrible trouble last night. We wandered into the kitchen early in the evening and found a huge plateful of delicious sandwiches on the table. We ate the middles out of half a dozen and then the Upright in Trousers came into the room. He shouted and threw a towel at us.

To avoid further trouble Thomasina and I left and went outside.

From underneath the lilac tree we then watched an apparently endless stream of visitors arrive. They were all elegantly dressed, they parked their cars all over the lawn and they carried gifts with them. Our Uprights were clearly having a party of some kind.

Thomasina suggested that in order to make our peace with the Upright in Trousers we should take in a small gift of our own. So I caught a plump and rather succulent looking fieldmouse and Thomasina picked up a bedraggled looking vole with a limp.

I don't think one should ever expect too much enthusiasm when arriving with a gift but I have to admit that we were both rather startled by the reception we got. The Upright who wears a Skirt started to scream and jumped up onto a chair. Someone else knocked over a tray full of glasses and a strange Upright whom I'd never seen before fainted. The Upright in Trousers then completely spoiled the mood of what promised to be a spectacular party by chasing the pair of us round the living room and threatening Thomasina with a large ladle.

In the end Thomasina and I decided that it was all far too exciting for us. We left our presents and went outside to spend the rest of the night in the garage.

When we woke up this morning all the cars had gone

and it was raining. I hate rain. Rain means mud.

I hate mess too and the inside of the house was in a terrible state. There were at least a dozen empty bottles lying on the floor in the living room and piles of dirty cups, plates and glasses in the kitchen. The sink was absolutely overflowing with them. Worst of all our food dish was quite empty.

Showing a remarkable level of patience both Thomasina and I sat and waited.

After two hours of hunger we crept upstairs to where the Uprights sleep. Normally I can wake them easily. A purr in the ear will usually do the trick. But they were both sleeping far too soundly to be woken so easily.

Full of despair, but absolutely empty of food, Thomasina and I went back downstairs again and made our way through into the kitchen. The plate of sandwiches that we'd started the night before was still sitting on the kitchen table. The pile was by no means as high as it had been the previous evening but there were still a dozen or so sandwiches waiting to be eaten. Desperate with hunger we jumped up onto the table and started to help ourselves.

Unfortunately, the plate was rather close to the edge and in our haste and excitement we knocked it off onto the floor. The crash was terrifyingly loud. Thomasina and I froze. At first I thought we might have got away with it but after a couple of minutes the Upright in Trousers came staggering downstairs in his pyjamas. I expected him to be furious but he looked at the plateful of scattered sandwiches and the broken plate, bent down and rubbed the side of my neck, murmured something affectionate and then went back upstairs again leaving us to help ourselves to the sandwiches!

Thomasina and I looked at one another and shrugged. I've never understood Uprights and I don't think I ever will.

January 2nd

The Uprights who live next door have acquired a dog. For the first few days the creature paid us remarkably little attention but slowly he has become bolder. Yesterday he barked persistently every time we went out into the garden. He terrified my half sister Thomasina who has always been rather frightened by dogs.

Today I decided that the dog must be taught a lesson. So while Thomasina stayed indoors well out of the way I went down to the bottom of the garden and sat on a fence post where it could see me.

Inevitably the dog's response was to try and jump up and catch me. But since the fence post was five feet up in the air I was perfectly safe.

I stayed up there for twenty minutes or so to get the dog in quite a rage and then I jumped down onto the flower border on our side of the fence. Just at this point there is a small hole in the fence, nowhere near large enough for a dog to get through but plenty large enough for him to use as a peep hole.

Naturally the dog got even more excited when he saw that I was down at ground level. He barked, scratched and whined and did a considerable amount of damage to the flower border on his side of the fence.

Eventually one of the neighbouring Uprights came down the garden path to see what was the matter. When he saw the mess that the dog had made he was absolutely furious. Through the fence I heard the dog whimpering pitifully.

Thomasina has been well avenged.

January 3rd

The dog next door has now been tethered to a large stake in the centre of the lawn. I spent a pleasant half an hour running up and down the top of the fence between our gardens. The stupid animal tried to follow me but ended up winding his lead round and round the stake. After thirty minutes the dog's lead was no more than a yard long and the wretched animal had become a prisoner of his own stupidity. Eventually I just sat while he barked and whimpered.

"I sat while the dog barked and whimpered."

I am glad that I am not a dog. They are such unintelligent animals.

January 4th

A good day today. I caught two mice, a shrew and a vole with a squint.

George is by far the wisest cat I know. He doesn't have a home but lives by his wits. He is jet black, very handsome and extremely athletic. I've seen him leap straight up onto the top of a six foot high fence. Thomasina and I have learnt a great deal from George.

After I'd told George about the fun we'd had with the dog next door he told me about an experience he once had with a vicious Alsatian.

"At the time I was living with some Uprights who didn't feed me very well," he began. "There wasn't much wildlife around and so I used to have to do a lot of dustbin scavenging. When you've got your head in a dustbin it's difficult to see what's happening behind you and on several occasions I very nearly got caught by a local Alsatian. Once I had to drop half a fillet of plaice that I'd found in order to escape. I hadn't had anything to eat for days and I was absolutely starving. By the time I got back to the dustbin the fish had gone."

"Eventually I decided that I had to teach the Alsatian a lesson," George continued. "I watched him carefully and quickly realised that there was one part of his regular routine that offered me an excellent opportunity to get my revenge. Every Sunday morning the dog used to trot to the local newsagents and pick up the Sunday papers. He would then bring them back home gripped firmly between his teeth."

George paused for a moment to lick the hair on his chest. I waited patiently for him to continue.

"I waited for him to come back home carrying the newspapers," George went on when he was satisfied with his chest hairs. "I picked a spot where there were several huge puddles and jumped right out in front of him. It went exactly according to plan. The Alsatian opened his mouth to bark at me and dropped the newspapers into a huge, murky puddle."

George purred with satisfaction at the memory of it.

"I bet he got into terrible trouble when he got home," he said. "Dogs are noisy but they are wonderfully stupid."

January 9th

One thing in particular annoys me about our Uprights. They will insist on giving Thomasina and I our meals in the same bowl.

I don't know why they do it.

They don't eat off the same dish. Why do they expect us to share a dish?

It is terribly annoying.

It's not that I find it unhygienic. I'm quite happy to eat whatever Thomasina is eating and her tongue is just as clean as mine. And it's not that she eats more than her fair share (which, if I'm honest, I have to say she does) because there is usually enough for me.

It's just that the bowl isn't quite big enough for two heads and one of these days we're going to end up getting our heads jammed together. And that will be embarrassing for everyone.

To avoid this awful possibility I have decided that in future I will take my meals after Thomasina has finished eating.

January 12th

When I woke up this morning the whole house was shaking. I thought something terrible was about to happen and so I immediately woke Thomasina and we darted outside.

But from outside everything seemed perfectly normal. There was no sign of anything terrible happening.

Since it was raining we both went back inside again quite quickly.

The house was still shaking. And the noise seemed to be coming from upstairs.

So, stealthily and courageously, Thomasina and I made our way up the stairs. From the landing it was clear that the noise and the vibrations were coming from the Upright's bedroom. So with Thomasina following I pushed open the bedroom door and slipped inside.

I had a tremendous shock. And so, I think, did Thomasina.

Sitting on a bicycle, wearing only his pyjamas, was the Upright in Trousers. It was an extraordinary sight. His face was red and flushed, his legs were pounding up and down and the bedroom floor was shaking and shuddering.

All that was remarkable enough. But the really strange thing was that the bicycle didn't have wheels.

And the Upright in Trousers was getting absolutely nowhere.

It made a very strange sight. Indeed it was too much for Thomasina and myself. We turned and left the bedroom as quietly as we had entered.

I asked Thomasina if she had any idea what the Upright was doing.

She shook her head and said that she didn't have the faintest idea. So we went downstairs, got outside and set off in search of George.

George, when we finally found him, seemed not in the least surprised.

"Oh, Uprights are always doing crazy things like that," he told us. "He was probably exercising."

Thomasina looked at me and I looked at Thomasina.

"What do you mean?" asked Thomasina. "And why didn't the bicycle have any wheels?"

"Uprights sometimes think that they aren't getting enough exercise," said George. "So the Upright wasn't cycling to get anywhere, he was cycling to get fit."

7

"I had a tremendous shock. It was an extraordinary sight."

"I don't understand," said Thomasina.

"It's because they worry about their health a lot," explained George.

"Oh,' said Thomasina. "I think I can understand that. But I don't understand why our Upright has started using a bicycle without any wheels. Up until about a month ago he used to ride to work on a bicycle. But then he bought a car. And now he drives to work."

"But don't you see?" said George. "When he was cycling to work he didn't need the extra exercise. But now that he isn't cycling to work he does!"

"I think I must be very stupid," said Thomasina. "But I still don't really understand."

I didn't say anything. But to be honest I don't understand either.

January 14th

I was washing myself this morning when I discovered a tick. I spent ages trying to get it off but it just wouldn't budge. In the end I decided that I'd have to get help from the Uprights. They're sure to know how to get rid of it.

January 17th

For over an hour and a half I'd been patiently waiting for a mouse to come from underneath the garden shed. I hadn't moved at all and although I was stiff with cramp and desperate to scratch my ear I was determined not to give in. I'd seen the mouse dive for cover and I knew that it couldn't see me. Before long it was bound to try and run for it. When it did I'd be ready for it.

And then suddenly "wham"!

One minute I was concentrating on the spot where I knew the mouse should reappear and the next minute I was rolling over and over on the soft earth.

At first I thought that I had been attacked. I had my claws out and was ready to defend myself from my unknown assailant when I suddenly realised who it was.

It was none other than dear old Penelope, one of our nearest neighbours. I quickly drew in my claws so that

I wouldn't hurt her, then I tapped her on the side of her head with my right paw before baring my teeth and taking a big soft bite at the skin underneath her chin.

Penelope squealed a little, struggled for a brief moment and then lay quite still. Penelope is no fighter.

"What on earth did you do that for?" I demanded angrily. "I could have got that mouse." I looked back towards the garden shed. I had no doubt that the mouse would have escaped while my attention had been diverted.

"It was just a bit of fun," said Penelope, rather hurt. "What are you getting so upset about?"

"I was about to catch my first mouse for two days," I told her. "That's what's the matter."

"You?" said Penelope, genuinely surprised. "Catch a mouse? I didn't know you were a hunter."

"Of course I'm a hunter!" I told her. "I could earn my keep if I really had to."

"I thought it was only toms who hunted," said Penelope, still puzzled.

"They may make the best hunters," I admitted. "But that doesn't mean that *we* can't hunt. I once caught four mice in one night."

Penelope looked terribly impressed. 'Could I learn to hunt?'' she asked me.

"I expect so," I said. "Anyone can hunt," I added rashly and probably inaccurately.

"Will you teach me," she asked, eagerly.

"Of course," I agreed, with thoughtless generosity.

And so I find that I am committed to teaching dear Penelope how to catch mice.

January 20th

After a considerable amount of effort I finally managed to get the Uprights to find my tick. As luck would have it the Upright who wears a Skirt was the one to make the discovery. Predictably she overreacted and ran off screaming for the Upright in Trousers. You'd have thought she'd found a crocodile in the bath.

There was much discussion about just what to do to get the tick off. Eventually the Upright in Trousers said that he'd heard someone say that a lighted cigarette end was the best way to remove the tick. Neither of them smoke but they managed to find half a packet of cigarettes left behind after last year's Christmas party and after a considerable amount of coughing and wheezing the Upright in Trousers managed to get one lit.

"I nearly fainted as the Upright in Trousers started splashing gin onto me."

To say that it didn't work is probably the understatement of the year. I ended up with a second degree burn. The Upright in Trousers ended up with an asthmatic attack. And the tick remained unmoved.

Next, the Upright who wears a Skirt suggested pulling

the tick out with a pair of tweezers. I tried to let them know that just pulling it wouldn't work but, of course, they had to try. The tick still didn't move.

By this time we were all quite distraught. I don't know what they were getting so upset about. It was me that was getting all the pain. The Upright who wears a Skirt decided to get advice and telephone another Upright. I could hear them talking about me.

Heaven knows what she was told but a few moments later I nearly fainted as the Upright in Trousers started splashing gin onto me. I'm not sure whether this was designed to get me unconscious so that I wouldn't feel the pain or to get the tick drunk so that it didn't hold on quite so tight. Whatever the rationale behind the procedure it worked. And the tick was removed.

At the end of it all I was absolutely exhausted. It isn't as if a tick is worth all that much bother. They always fall off after two or three weeks when they've had their fill. And apart from being a bit of a nuisance they don't really do much harm.

If I get another tick I shall do my best to see that the Uprights don't find it.

January 24th

Penelope had her first hunting lesson today. I do hope that it was not an omen for the future.

I don't wish to be unkind but I think that Penelope is going to have real difficulty catching anything that can still move. If I spend two hours a day for the next year instilling her with the fundamentals then it is just possible, *just* possible mark you, that she will be able to catch a stuffed mouse by next summer. But I wouldn't bet on it. She seems genetically incapable of stalking. She forgets to put her claws out when she pounces. She makes a noise like a lawn mower when she's moving through the grass and she has absolutely no patience at all. Nor does she have any "killer" instinct. When I showed her the carcase of a mouse I'd caught a couple of days ago she was quite upset.

January 27th

For months I've wondered what lies behind the door at the top of the stairs. Several times I've seen the Upright who wears a Skirt open it and go inside for a few moments. On each occasion she has either taken towels or linen into the room or else she has brought towels and linen out of the room. One or twice I tried to slip in between her legs but each time she succeeded in keeping me out.

But today the door was left open and I managed to get inside.

It was a magnificent experience. And despite what happened later it was one that I wouldn't want to have missed.

Most of the room, which was extremly small, was taken up with a huge cushion covered metal tank. The tank was boiling hot and the cushions that surrounded it were uncomfortably warm to the touch.

I couldn't help thinking how silly it was to put so much effort into heating such a tiny room that is hardly ever used. But then, as George has pointed out on many occasions, Uprights aren't the most logical creatures on this earth.

Directly above the metal tank there was a slatted wooden shelf upon which were piled several dozen neatly folded towels, pillow cases and sheets.

At first I couldn't work out how to climb up onto the shelf. But eventually I discovered that if I wriggled round to the back of the metal tank I could just manage to scramble up between the shelf and the wall. It was a tight

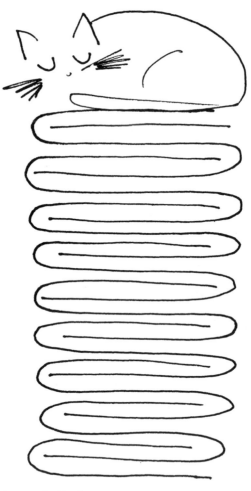

"Sleeping on a bed is pleasant enough. But this was very special."

fit but I was determined to see what it was like up there. And eventually I managed it.

It was wonderful.

Sleeping on a bed is pleasant enough. But this was

something very special. The pile of towels and sheets must have been at least two feet thick and the heat escaping from the large metal tank meant that even the towels on top of the pile were very cosy.

I curled up into my favourite position with my nose tucked under my tail and went to sleep.

And what wonderful dreams I had.

I don't know whether it was the fact that I was so comfortable and warm, or the fact that I was safe from prying eyes and Thomasina, but I had some of the best dreams I've ever had. I dreamt that I had a wonderful chase after a young rabbit in a beautiful meadow where the grass was soft and green and the sky plain bright blue. I dreamt that I caught the juiciest and crunchiest mouse in the world. And I dreamt that I was sitting in a garden where the air was thick with butterflies that couldn't fly more that two feet above the ground.

And then suddenly I started to dream that I was being chased by a crowd of angry Uprights all wearing hobnail boots and carrying huge sticks.

I ran and I ran and I ran as fast as I could but the Uprights with the Boots kept getting closer and closer. I wriggled and dodged and turned and scratched and clawed. But they caught me and held me down and started to kick me and stamp on my stomach. The pain from their heavy kicking was excruciating and unbearable.

And then I woke up.

My bladder was absolutely bursting and I was desperate to empty it.

I stretched and cautiously peered over the edge of the pile of towels upon which I was perched. It was pitch black in there which was strange because when I'd gone into the room I'd been able to see around me quite well.

Then I realised what had happened. While I'd been asleep someone had gone past and had pushed the door to. I was shut in.

Filled with pain and panic I leapt down from the shelf and landed clumsily on the floor below. That made the pain in my stomach a hundred times worse. I pushed and scratched at the door but I couldn't move it. It was shut firmly. So I scratched at the carpet and the paintwork hoping desperately that someone would hear me.

I was about to come to terms with the fact that disgrace and embarrassment was the only course of action available to me when the door opened. The Upright who wears a Skirt had heard the noise I'd been making and had opened the door for me.

Making suitably soothing and apologetic noises she bent down to pick me up. But I didn't have time for graceful greetings and nice apologies. I had to get outside as quickly as I possibly could. I sped between her legs and raced down the stairs at top speed.

February 1st

It has now been raining more or less non stop for three days. Apart from essential excursions Thomasina and I haven't been out of the house in that time. And to be perfectly honest I wouldn't be offended if our Uprights brought back the tray Thomasina and I used when we were small. The garden is a sea of mud and every time I have to go outside it takes me three quarters of an hour to get my paws clean again.

February 3rd

When I was small I used to find it difficult to differentiate between Uprights. But over the years I've found that one of the most reliable ways to tell them apart is by their smell.

Today the Upright who smells like a musk deer came round for tea.

16

I hate her.

Whenever she sees me she always insists on picking me up and holding me on her lap. She turns me over onto my back and scratches my tummy with her nails. I don't dislike any of this but all the time she makes incredibly silly noises that I suspect she thinks make her sound like a cat. In fact she just sounds like a musk deer pretending to be an Upright pretending to be a cat. It really is embarrassing.

Over the months I've tried all sorts of ploys to get away from her.

First, I tried darting out through the cat flap and hiding in the garden just as soon as I smelt her coming. But that didn't work. She just chased me round and round the garden. Not only do I hate being chased round the garden almost as much as I hate the noises she makes, but once she trod on a mouse run that I'd been keeping an eye on for a week. Spoiled my sport entirely.

When that didn't work I tried being sick on her lap. I really gave her the works. I dug my claws in deep to stop her throwing me off and brought up a disgusting mess of half digested hair balls and rabbit meaty lumps. You'd have thought she'd have got the message. Not a bit of it. These days she always brings an old towel to spread out on her lap. But she still makes her silly noises. And I still hate it. And her.

February 5th

I was teaching Penelope some basic hunting moves, with a large mouse as a target, when the Upright who wears a Skirt came by.

She was furious when she saw what I was doing and ran off to fetch the Upright in Trousers.

"Alice is playing with a mouse," I heard her say. "Can't you take it off her?"

17

He couldn't, of course. We disappeared behind the greenhouse with it. But the comment did annoy me. And it hurt a little too.

And even Penlope seemed a little confused.

"It does seem a bit cruel," she said as I clouted the mouse twice in rapid succession. "Especially when we get fed so well by our Uprights."

"Penelope, you must never forget that this isn't playing," I said to her. "This is hunting. And it is extremely important that you acquire and never lose good hunting skills."

"I don't understand," said Penelope.

I explained to her that cats don't hunt for fun or sport in the way that Uprights do. "Our hunting skills are vital," I told her. "As long as we can catch and kill our prey then we will always know that we can be independent."

"But we don't have to hunt," protested Penelope. "There are meals put out for us twice a day."

"That's exactly why it is so important that we carry on hunting and polishing our skills," I told her. "It's all very nice being provided with regular meals of tinned food. And like most cats if I'm honest I have to admit that I prefer a meal of tinned food to having to crunch up a live mouse. But if we couldn't catch our own food then we would be totally dependent on the Uprights."

Slowly the light seemed to dawn on Penelope. "I see what you mean," she said at last. "If we can catch our own food then we can choose whether or not we allow the Uprights to feed us. When we can't catch our own food then we are totally reliant on the Uprights feeding us. It changes everything doesn't it?"

"Exactly," I said. Pleased that she understood at last.

"But why do we have to practise killing the same mouse time and time again?" asked Penelope.

"We don't need to eat mice very often," I explained. "And yet we need to keep our hunting skills finely honed. We have a straight choice. Either we kill lots of mice

18

every day. Or we kill one and take our time over it to get all the practise we need from that one animal.''

"So really," said Penelope, "when the Uprights think we're playing with a mouse we're really trying to be kind to other mice."

"Exactly," I said. "I just wish that the Uprights would understand that."

February 7th

I do wish I could find out who keeps spreading myths about what cats can and can't do, and about what they do and don't like. Tonight it was the fish routine.

"We've got something really special for you," said the Upright who wears a Skirt.

"You'll love this," said the Upright in Trousers.

"I hate fish."

And so on and so on in much the same sort of vein for five minutes or more. I should have guessed of course.

19

But I always fall for it. I thought they'd got me something really special: a jar of meat paste or a bowl of cold custard, for example.

But no, it was a great white chunk of nasty, smelly cod.

I hate fish.

February 9th

Thomasina and I ran into the living room this evening feeling a little frisky. It was pouring down outside, and had been all day. So we thought we'd play tag around the furniture. It's one of our favourite indoor games.

But the Uprights weren't at all enthusiastic. In fact they both told us off. We got the strong impression that if we didn't keep still and quiet we'd be thrown outside. Since it was raining we were both happy to allow discretion to overcome valour.

The reason for all this was the fact that the Uprights were both busy watching and listening to the television.

The television has been a mystery to both Thomasina and myself ever since we've been living with our Uprights. It sits in one corner of the living room and never, ever moves. But it is very much alive. And it is very important. The Uprights always listen to it very respectfully and talk back to it only occasionally. And then, when they do talk back, they always look embarrassed, as though they feel foolish.

There are two things that are particularly odd about the television.

First, it talks in many different voices. Normally Thomasina and I can identify an Upright quickly by the sound it makes when talking. But the television seems able to speak in a thousand different tongues. Perhaps it is this skill which inspires so much respect from the Uprights.

Secondly, although the television is always warm when it is talking, it goes quite cold when it goes to sleep.

Neither Thomasina nor I understand this.

February 10th

Penelope's hunting lessons continue.

Today we nearly caught a shrew but Penelope got so excited that she started to purr loudly when the shrew was still a foot and a half away. What made things worse was the fact that the shrew seemed amused by this. I'll swear that he laughed at us before scampering away.

February 14th

Uprights fascinate me. I can sit and watch them for hours. And I often do.

But although I must have spent a good part of my life watching the things that Uprights do there are still many aspects of their lives that puzzle me.

Today the Upright in Trousers came into the house carrying a huge bunch of flowers and a box of chocolates. The Upright who wears a Skirt then proceeded to give him a big hug and smother him in kisses.

What on earth was all this about, I wonder?

What had inspired this sudden show of affection?

Uprights are, it seems to me, very social creatures and they seem unable to live without these outbursts of un-bridled affection. Thomasina and I are close, of course. But I'm sure we could both survive perfectly happily on our own.

We certainly don't need to bring each other dead mice or bundles of cat nip!

What an absolutely terrible day.

I knew it was going to be a bad day when I woke up and found that it had rained during the night and soaked the window seat in the Upright's bedroom. It hadn't rained on top of me but the damp patch had spread right across underneath where I had been lying. It is bound to have affected my joints. I expect I'll get all sorts of aches and pains.

Then, after breakfast, I went outside and found that the Upright in Trousers was tidying the garage.

I really hate it when he does that.

For the last few months I've been carefully tracking a whole range of possible targets. There were two mice living behind the old half-filled cans of paint that he had been storing just inside the door. And there were dozens of really large, meaty spiders hanging around by the window.

I don't know what inspires these sudden flashes of tidiness. But they occur at irregular and unpredictable intervals. And they are a fearful nuisance. The tidying disturbs all the wildlife that is living in the garage. And that isn't fair to the wildlife and it isn't fair to Thomasina and I who want to catch it all.

The last time the Uprights tidied up the garage every single mouse left and for six months afterwards you'd have had a job to find so much as a spider in there! Thomasina and I prefer hunting outdoors. But occasionally if it is raining or particularly cold we like to go in there for an hour's practice.

Not that it was only the hunting potential of the garage that was ruined by the tidying up process.

My sacking bed and Thomasina's old gardening trousers were both moved. I was really upset about the sacking and I suspect that Thomasina will be furious when she discovers that her trousers have gone. For over a year now I've frequently dozed on that piece of sacking.

Tucked away on a high shelf it gave me an excellent view of the whole garage and it was well away from all the draughts that are usually such a problem in any sort of outhouse. Over the months that piece of sacking had acquired a comfortable and extremely pleasant feel to it. It had been moulded to my body and had become thick with loose hairs.

But the worse thing that has happened is that the Upright in Trousers has mended the broken window! It was that Window which gave Thomasina and I our entry into the garage. All we had to do to get into the garage was to climb up onto the window sill (a very easy leap from the ground) and then scramble up and through the broken window. The exit from the garage was a little more difficult but quite manageable.

And now the Upright has replaced the broken window with a brand new window.

That effectively means that neither Thomasina nor I will ever be able to hunt in the garage again.

What a terrible blow this is.

February 23rd

This afternoon I continued with Penelope's hunting lessons. I caught a small fieldmouse behind the greenhouse, picked it up carefully and carried it back to the centre of the lawn where Penelope was waiting.

"There you are," I said. "Pretend you've caught the mouse. And now kill it."

Penelope looked at me aghast. "Kill it?" she said. "How?"

I just stared at her.

So, plucking up all her courage, she gently extended her neck, opened her jaws and started to bite the mouse on its flank. Not surprisingly the mouse turned and attacked Penelope's nose with its mouth and claws.

Penelope retreated quickly, tears mingling with a few specks of blood. She looked more surprised than hurt.

"That's your first lesson," I said. "Never try to bite your prey until you've stunned it." I reached out a paw and hit the mouse on its head. It lay still, dazed by the blow.

"How did you do that?" Penelope wanted to know.

"Like this," I said, repeating the movement. "Just hit it on the side of the head as hard as you can."

Penelope looked aghast. "Kill it?" she said. "How?"

"Now do I bite it?" asked Penelope, a trifle uncertainly.

"No," I said, quite firmly. "Now you wait."

She looked puzzled.

"It may just be pretending to be knocked out," I explained. "If you move too close it might bite you again."

"Oh," said Penelpe, backing away sharply.

"We wait a minute or two to see if it moves." I said. "And then we hit it again."

We waited a while and then I reached forward and smacked the mouse firmly on the side of its head. It didn't move.

"Shall I bite it now?" asked Penelope.

"Yes," I said. "But on its neck. And firmly. Just remember this is only a mouse, but one day you could be trying to kill a rat. You need to be decisive if you don't want to get hurt."

Looking apprehensive but strangely determined Penelope extended her neck, opened her jaws and bit.

She missed the mouse altogether and the crashing of her jaws would have wakened Sleeping Beauty.

After a momentary pause she tried again. This time she succeeded in biting a chunk out of the mouse's neck.

I half expected her to spit out the piece she'd bitten off. But she didn't. She chewed at it, cautiously at first, and then with slowly growing enthusiasm.

After she'd finished her eyes lit up and her whiskers twitched appreciatively.

"I'd never realised that there was meat inside," she said. "Fresh meat too. I thought meat only came in tins."

February 27th

I've found another tick. I can't see it properly but this one is on my back. I spent ages trying to think where I could have caught it. All I can think is that it got its jaws into me when I was romping around in the long grass down by the blackcurrants. I shan't go down there again in a hurry. They say you can't get ticks simply from a roll in the long grass but now I know that to be untrue.

Anyway, the main problem now is to hide the tick from the Uprights until it falls off by itself. I really don't fancy them trying their removal procedures again.

March 7th

I've been reading back through my diary. And I've just found the entry for February 14th.

When I wrote that day's entry I said that Uprights seem to be very sociable creatures and that I couldn't understand why they showered each other with gifts and affection.

Well, I think I understand now though it took Thomasina's illness to really bring it home to me.

Over the many months that we have lived together Thomasina and I have argued many, many times.

She sometimes annoys me a great deal. For example, when I'm having a snooze in a sunny spot she'll often come over and want to play. She'll jump on me and playfully bite my ear. It drives me crazy but I know that she doesn't mean any harm. She's got a very playful personality and she finds it difficult to lie down and do nothing.

But although we do argue a lot we have grown very close. And I know that if I'm ever in trouble Thomasina will come and help me.

I remember once, a little over a year ago, when I was a young and foolish cat, hardly more than a kitten really, and I got stuck up a tree.

It was entirely my own fault. I'd been chasing a bird (in those days I was always chasing birds) with excessive enthusiasm. I'd gone up far higher than I should have gone. I really was stuck. I don't mind admitting it now but I was terrified. I don't really like heights all that much but as long as I'm moving I'm usually all right. But I couldn't go up and I couldn't get down. I could see myself being stuck there for ever.

And then Thomasina came along. She could see straight away that I was stuck and she knew exactly what to do. I was panicking, but she didn't panic for one minute. She ran straight indoors and found the Upright in Trousers. And then she miaowed loudly at him. She

26

miaowed so loudly that I could hear her even though I was half way up a tree down at the bottom of the garden. She wouldn't stop until he abandoned what he was doing and followed her out of the house and down the garden.

The Upright in Trousers got me down with a ladder and I've been grateful to him ever since. But it was Thomasina who went and fetched him for me. Without her the chances are that no one would have ever found me. I'd have died up that tree. My sisterly affection for Thomasina really began to flourish on that day.

But it took her recent illness to make me realise just how much Thomasina really means to me.

It started suddenly. One day she was absolutely fine. Indeed, she caught two shrews and a mouse that day. And then the next day she could hardly move. I came downstairs one morning and found her lying flat out on the sofa coughing her heart out. It was a terrible sight and I felt guilty because I had not heard her coughing during the night. Her head was stretched forward and her body was wracked by a series of terrible, heaving spasms.

I had only been downstairs for a moment or two when the Upright in Trousers appeared. He was as concerned as I was. He knelt down and gently stroked her head. Valiant as ever she tried to respond. But the effort was too much for her. It simply started another coughing attack.

After calling up to the Upright who wears a Skirt the Upright in Trousers went straight to the telephone. I could hear him explaining that Thomasina was ill and needed help.

It was over an hour before the Upright who smells of Antiseptic arrived and it was the longest hour of my life. I stayed close to her but Thomasina seemed to be drifting away from me. And I didn't want her to go. I licked her face to let her know that I was there. She tried to nuzzle against me but she was so weak that her head hardly moved, despite the apparent effort she made.

Four days it took for her to recover. Four days during which I hardly left her side. The Uprights wanted to keep me in another room. But I wouldn't let them. I scratched and miaowed so much that they had to let me back in again.

The nights were the worst. I thought that Thomasina was going to die. But our Uprights were wonderful. They went upstairs to sleep as usual but came down every hour or so to see how she was.

I shall never forget the joy I felt when I began to realise that she was going to live. The Upright who wears a Skirt had prepared a dish of sardines and milk and that was the first food Thomasina ate.

Now I understand why the Uprights show each other affection and give each other presents. There is a joy in true love and real friendship that cannot be over-valued.

March 9th

At last Penelope has caught something more or less by herself. We were hunting near the dustbins at the back of the fish and chip shop when a vole popped its head out of the ground no more than two inches in front of her. She quickly dazed it with a remarkably effective sideways blow. But she was far too enthusiastic and instead of enjoying a good hunting game we found ourselves with a freshly killed corpse on our hands.

Penelope was thrilled by her first real kill. Even though I warned her that voles do not usually taste very nice she insisted on eating it. She said that it was the first meal she'd ever prepared with her own paws and she wasn't going to miss it, whatever it tasted like.

She was sick three times on the way home.

March 10th

Thomasina ran into the house today in a terrible state. She said that she'd just seen a rat which had teeth all over its body. I thought she was exaggerating but was intensely curious to see just what she had found so I cautiously led the way back outside into the garden again. Thomasina kept several yards behind me and checked constantly that her route back to the cat flap was not impeded.

"It looks harmless enough to me," I told her.

"Just try hitting it on the head," suggested Thomasina.

"Where is its head?" I asked her. "And where is its tail?"

"Where is its head?" I asked her. "And where is its tail?"

"I haven't the foggiest," said Thomasina. "But if you don't believe me that it's got teeth all over its body just try giving it a pat."

Cautiously I extended a paw and tapped it gently.

It bit me.

I retreated a yard or two, licked my paw and watched

it carefully. It didn't move. It didn't attack and it didn't try to run away.

"I'm going to try again," I told Thomasina.

"Be careful!" she implored.

Stealthily I crept back and tapped it on its back again.

It bit me again.

Neither Thomasina nor I had ever seen a headless rat that could bite before.

We both decided that we were feeling desperately hungry so we turned and sped for the cat flap and the kitchen.

March 11th

The fattest Upright in the world came to tea today. I sometimes wonder how Uprights manage to get so fat. I've always found it remarkably simple to keep my figure. I eat when I am hungry and I stop when I am not. What more is there to it?

Still, although I don't know why Uprights get so fat, I'm glad they do. I doubt if there is anything in the world quite so comfortable as a large, fat, spacious lap. On a thinner lap you have to put up with bony protrubrances. A fat lap is wonderfully comfortable.

March 14th

Penelope has had kittens!

March 17th

The Uprights had left a large empty cardboard box in the middle of the living room this afternoon. It didn't smell of anything particularly interesting but I knew when I saw it that Thomasina wouldn't be able to resist it.

Sure enough, when she came in an hour or so later she went straight for it and jumped inside without even a cautious sniff.

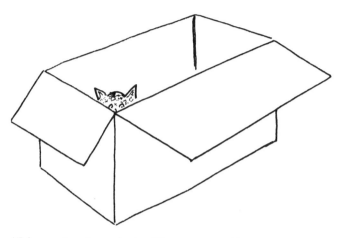

"I knew when I saw it that Thomasina wouldn't be able to resist it."

She is the most curious and incautious cat I have ever known and one of these days she is going to jump straight into trouble.

That box could have been full of any number of dangers.

"But it wasn't," she said, when I remonstrated with her a little later.

"Why do you like cardboard boxes so much?" I asked her. "You can never resist a cardboard box, can you?"

Thomasina just shrugged. "I don't know," she said. "Why do you like cold custard so much?"

Isn't that a silly thing to say?

There is no comparison.

March 18th

"It was a hedgehog," said George with a laugh when we'd explained what we'd seen the other day. "They're covered in hundreds and hundreds of needle sharp spines."

"What are they for?" asked Thomasina.

"I don't know what they're for," replied George. "But I shouldn't worry. Even if you could kill a hedgehog you'd never find a way to eat it."

March 20th

For twelve months now I have sharpened and cleaned my claws on the trunk of a large lilac tree. The bark had just the right texture to it. But this morning I went out into the garden and found that the Upright in Trousers had chopped the tree down. What a tragedy.

March 23rd

I hate making small decisions.

The big decisions – like where to sleep at night and whether to go out hunting or sit by the fire – are easy to make. I just let instinct take over.

But the small decisions are more difficult.

Today I spent ten minutes staring at a sycamore tree and an oak tree trying to decide which to use as a replacement for my lilac tree. In the end I couldn't decide so I gave up and went hunting. But I didn't catch anything. Probably because I was still worrying about which tree to use to sharpen my claws.

March 26th

I worry about the Uprights. I do wish they would learn
to relax properly. This evening, for example, the Upright
in Trousers sat down for what he said was going to be
a relaxing evening in front of the television.

For the first ten minutes he sat quite still. I was so
impressed that I jumped onto his lap.

Then he started to fidget. He wanted to read his newspaper. Then he wanted to write a letter to someone. Then
he wanted a cup of tea. Then he wanted a biscuit.

After half an hour of this I gave up and went to sit
by the fire.

The Upright who wears a Skirt isn't a lot better.

March 27th

Lapsong II came by today to show us the latest new collar
that her Upright had bought her. Personally, I thought
it rather cheap and gaudy. It is made out of blue shiny
leatherette and is studded with small stones of indetermi-
nate origin. It looks the sort of thing that might be accep-
table around the dustbins behind the local cinema.

I told her that I thought it suited her perfectly. She,
poor sweet innocent thing, seemed pleased by my comment.

I've only known Lapsong II for about two weeks. I
met her more or less by accident.

About half an hour's gentle stroll away from our home
there is a huge estate protected by a high brick wall.
The grounds stretch for miles in all directions and the
house is magnificent. Surprisingly, perhaps, Lapsong II
is the only feline occupant of this remarkable house.

When I first met her I was in the stable hunting a mem-
ber of a particularly speedy family of mice. I thought
it had managed to wriggle underneath an old loose floor-

"Lapsong II came by to show us her latest collar. Personally, I thought it rather cheap and gaudy."

board and following the noise it was making (there isn't much chance of following anything by its smell in a stable) I had, so I thought, got it cornered behind a bale of straw.

But when I leapt over the straw bale I suddenly found myself on top of a neatly combed and manicured Siamese cat. I was, to say the least, startled.

That was my first meeting with Lapsong II.

It seemed that Lapsong II's other reason for calling today was to tell us that her Uprights have just had their home double-glazed. I pointed out that I could not possibly understand what advantage such a development could offer, but Lapsong II saw the alterations merely as a sign of enviable wealth and status. It seems that the extra panes of glass are designed not so much to keep the cold winds out but to keep other Uprights envious.

It became quite clear during our conversation that Lapsong II not only has tremendous respect for her Uprights, but also considers them to be vastly superior to her in evolutionary terms.

"I do so admire their inherited skills and acquired judgements," she told us. "Uprights have such powers and such a wealth of abilities."

I was puzzled by this, for although I have affection for Uprights I have never been unduly impressed by any powers they possess. I asked Lapsong II to explain more fully what she meant.

"Just think about it for a moment or two," she insisted. "Uprights can do all sorts of things that you and I cannot even attempt."

I asked her to be a little more specific.

"Well," said Lapsong II after a moment or two's thought, "they can open tins."

I fear I failed to disguise the fact that I was not impressed by this.

"They can ride bicycles," she went on. "They have a well developed sense of balance."

"But I can balance on a window ledge," I pointed out. "I can jump out of windows, I can jump up onto the top of the bathroom cabinet and I can lick my bottom."

For a moment Lapsong II seemed nonplussed by this. She had to admit that she had never seen an Upright do any of these things.

"But their lives are filled with so much *meaning*," she said forcefully. "Often when they come home at night they are so exhausted that they can hardly move. They set off every morning without exception. Even though they may sometimes moan a little they are so dedicated to their work that they subjugate their personal preferences to what they undoubtedly see as their greater responsibilites."

"But what is it all for?" I demanded.

"It is all part of their superior lifestyle," explained

Lapsong II. "They are, in evolutionary terms, far more advanced than any cat can ever hope to be."

I think I have slowly come to understand some of what Lapsong II was saying.

We have no real responsibilities in our lives. We sit around all day. We sleep. We lie in the sun. We eat. We play. We sleep a little more. Even though we are perfectly capable of looking after ourselves we allow the Uprights to look after us. If the Uprights had not evolved then we would have to find our own shelter, we would have to hunt for all our own food every day and we would have no one to care for us, clean up after us or nurse us.

I am indeed convinced that evolution is an excellent thing. Though I confess that I am glad that I myself have not had to evolve.

March 30th

I'd been outside for most of the day when it suddenly started to rain.

When I ran indoors I had the shock of my life.

The whole living room had been changed around.

I thought at first that I had run into the wrong house.

But all the smells were right. There was the sofa that Thomasina sleeps on. And the chair that I like.

And I could smell both our Uprights.

I went back into the kitchen just to make sure that I was in the right house. And sure enough everything was there in the right place. The kitchen table was still in the middle of the floor. And our food bowls and water bowl were still by the side of the Cold Cupboard.

I went back into the living room and looked around slowly.

Everything had moved.

The sofa and the chairs and the tables were all in

36

different positions. And the carpet smelt very strange. It smelt a bit like the Upright who wears a Skirt when she has been in the bathroom for hours.

When the Upright in Trousers came in a little later he had a shock too. I could tell that he didn't know what to make of it. But he recovered well and put a brave face on it. When the Upright who wears a Skirt came into the room he went over to her and said how nice it all looked.

I'm still not sure why everything has been moved. But if he doesn't mind then I don't really see why I should. After all, it isn't as if anything important has actually disappeared.

March 31st

George invited Thomasina and I to accompany him on a hunting trip this evening. He told us that he had found a garden about a quarter of a mile away where the Uprights have built a pond and stocked it with dozens of goldfish.

It was the first time either Thomasina or I have been fishing.

George said that the best way to catch fish is to lie down close to the pond's edge and to put one paw just below the surface of the water. Then, when a goldfish swims by, it is possible to reach out and ''strike'' without splashing and alarming the fish unduly.

It was amazing to watch him at work. Within the space of no more than five minutes he successfully hooked three good sized fish out of the water. Thomasina and I were both very impressed.

But it was only when Thomasina and I tried that we realised just how skilled George really was. When

"Within the space of no more than five minutes George had success-fully hooked three fish out of the water."

Thomasina tried to catch her first fish she made the mistake of holding her paw just above the surface of the water rather than just below it. I suspect that she did this because she hates getting her fur wet and she wanted to delay the dreadful moment for as long as possible.

The result was that when she struck down at her chosen fish the splash that her paw made startled the fish so much that it swam away. To make matters worse Thomasina had put so much effort behind her strike that when her paw failed to collide with the fish she overbalanced. She didn't fall completely into the pool but the whole of her right front leg and right shoulder got absolutely soaked. So too did her face and head from the splash that she made.

I tried next.

And I am afraid that I was no more successful than Thomasina. I did manage to scratch the side of the fish but all I obtained for my trouble were a few scales underneath my claws.

George was very kind. He said that fishing was an acquired skill and that we shouldn't feel too bad about it. He said he'd give us one more demonstration before we tried again.

"Then," he said, "we'll have a splendid fish supper."

But before George could move back into position by the pond there was a strange noise behind us.

Both Thomasina and I looked round but could see nothing.

But George knew exactly what it was.

"Follow me," he hissed. "As fast as you can."

Thomasina and I hesitated for just a moment but the tone of George's voice told us that we should obey him without question. So we ran, jumped the garden fence and disappeared among the long grasses in the next door neighbour's garden.

As we lay there in the long grass Thomasina and I looked at George with some surprise. George is one of the bravest cats I know. He isn't the sort of fellow to run away without just cause. We both wanted to know what the danger was.

"The Upright who lives there has an airgun," explained George. "I've been hit once or twice and it stings." He explained that the Upright shoots from one of his bedroom windows and never gives any warning. "When he misses you can hear the pellets hissing through the air and then plopping into the earth," explained George. He sighed and shook his head. "What a shame," he said sadly, "I left three fish on the grass all ready for eating."

Thomasina and I expressed our disappointment but told him that we had at least enjoyed the lesson and were grateful for the opportunity to watch him in action.

I didn't mention the fact that I don't like fish. Somehow I suspect that George would not have understood.

April 2nd

Penelope's kittens have acquired many of her mannerisms and watching her kittens follow her across the lawn today I was reminded of a lovely story about a cat called Lavinia who lived not far from here five or six years ago. I was told this story by George and so I'm sure it's true.

When she was young Lavinia was involved in a rather nasty car accident on the busy road outside the house where she lived. She was run over and badly crushed and as a result lost her left front paw and part of her left front foreleg. Consequently she walked on her three good legs. As she walked (or half walked and half hopped) she kept the stump of her left foreleg held in front of her, partly to keep it out of the way and partly to use it to help her retain her balance.

By the time she got pregnant for the first time Lavinia had grown perfectly accustomed to her own rather unusual gait. Neither she nor any of her friends nor the Uprights who lived with her thought there was anything in the slightest bit unusual about the way she moved.

But Lavinia's friends and Uprights were surprised when they saw the way that Lavinia's kittens walked.

For every single one of them walked in exactly the same way that Lavinia walked. Even though they all had four perfect limbs they all walked with their left front forelegs and paws held high in front of them. They had learned to mimic Lavinia's strange, half walking, half hopping gait.

And according to George they all continued to walk like that even when they had grown up. And what's more, exactly the same thing happened to the subsequent kittens that Lavinia gave birth to.

"It was wonderful," said George. "You could always tell one of Lavinia's kittens when you saw it."

"I've often wondered," he mused, "whether or not when her kittens had kittens they too walked in that rather unusual way."

April 3rd

There were visiting Uprights here today. The Upright in Trousers was obviously keen to impress them. He scurried around making them drinks and giving them snacks and generally being attentive.

I felt so sorry for him that when he wanted to impress them by calling me over to sit on his lap I responded. He seemed really pleased and I felt good about it. He stroked my back, tickled me under the chin and told everyone there what a splendid cat I was.

But then one of the visiting Uprights wanted another drink and the Upright in Trousers picked me up and put me down on the floor simply so that he could attend to this insignificant request. I was not well pleased.

So when he sat down again and called me over to him I deliberately ignored him. Indeed, to rub in my displeasure, and to make sure that he realised exactly how I felt, I went and sat on the lap of a very elderly Upright with a shiny head.

I didn't stay long. He smelt of burning vegetation.

April 4th

Our Upright in Trousers spent the day at home today. Thomasina and I dread him having a day around the house. He seems quite incapable of having a pleasant, relaxed day without trying to rebuild the house or redesign the garden.

When I first realised that he was going to hang around I went outside to try and find a little peace and quiet down at the bottom of the garden. But I'd not been there more than twenty minutes when he appeared with a pile of old newspapers, a piece of old carpet and a box of matches. The stench from the resultant bonfire would have been enough to scare away anyone.

Retreating from the bottom of the garden I made my way into the garden shed. There is a huge family of mice living in the garden shed and it is an excellent hunting ground. I'd just got myself settled on an old jumper when the Upright in Trousers came rushing in to escape a short, sharp shower. He decided to have a clear out. If there is anything I hate it is spring cleans and clear outs. All the best trails were destroyed, three out of seven mouse runs were destroyed, four mouse nesting sites were disturbed and my favourite jumper was thrown out.

First the garage and now the shed. Is nothing sacred?

From the garden shed I went indoors and settled down on the sofa. I swear that I hadn't been there for more than ten minutes when he came in and switched on the television. Normally I don't mind the television at all. It keeps the Uprights amused for hours. But in the middle of the afternoon? I found it very annoying.

And so it went on. I have noticed before that the Uprights are at their most troublesome when they haven't got enough to do. The truth is that they get bored far too easily and just aren't very good at idling.

By late afternoon I'd been back outside twice and had still failed to find any peace. I decided to go upstairs and lie down on the bed, thinking that I'd be safe there. Surely, I thought, the Uprights won't come into the bedroom in the daytime, however bored they get.

I couldn't have been more wrong. Within half an hour the two Uprights had come into the bedroom and climbed into bed. In broad daylight! At first I was determined

42

to sit it out but it was like trying to get to sleep in a rowing boat in a hurricane. I gave up and went back outside to the rhododendron bush at the bottom of the garden.

I do hope that he doesn't decide to have many more unexpected days at home.

April 6th

The Uprights bought us a large tin of pilchards today.
    At first I thought they were fish.
    They look like fish. And they smell like fish.
    But they can't be fish. Because I like them.

April 8th

Oscar really isn't the most popular of cats. He's the sort of tom who will eat a shrew (even though he absolutely hates the taste) rather than leave it lying around where another cat might have a little fun playing with it. He's not too particular about his personal hygiene either, and when it comes to a fight he's an out and out coward.

But despite all those faults he is a cat. And none of us like to see a cat having a hard time. And poor old Oscar certainly has a hard time of it.

He lives with one of the most unpleasant Uprights I've ever met: an elderly, bad tempered former policeman. Apparently he only agreed to share his home with Oscar (that's the way *he* sees it!) because he was having trouble with mice. He treats poor Oscar abominably. He never allows him into the house at night. He never gives him any food or water. He never shows him any sign of affection or respect.

Poor old Oscar. It's perhaps hardly surprising that he has hardly any of the usual social graces.

For months now Oscar has been talking of running away. But he's never really had the courage to do it.

But suddenly, two days ago, Oscar finally made the final decision. None of us know exactly what happened. Some say that his Upright found mouse droppings in the kitchen and beat poor Oscar with an old shoe.

Anyway, whatever the truth of it might be, Oscar made his final decision. He was determined to leave.

"I don't know why it's taken me so long to make my mind up," he said. "But now that I've finally made the decision I feel free."

It was George who suggested that he wait for a while.

"He sounds a really unpleasant person, your Upright," said George to Oscar.

Oscar nodded sadly.

"And he really hates mice?"

"He certainly does," agreed Oscar. "Mice, rats, shrews, voles, moles – he can't stand any of them. That's the only reason he didn't throw me out."

"Then we should teach him a lesson," said George.

"What do you mean?" asked Oscar, puzzled.

And George outlined his plan. It was brilliantly conceived, on that we all agreed. And I'll swear that poor old Oscar had tears in his eyes when he heard us all agree to take part in George's scheme.

Oscar told us that his Upright is going away for a few weeks. When he gets back we will put George's plan into operation.

April 10th

This afternoon I went round to see how Penelope is getting on with her kittens. I fear that she is not proving to be much of a mother.

All the time I was there her three kittens behaved in a most irresponsible and disrespectful manner, but not once did Penelope admonish them. One expects kittens to do a certain amount of playful romping but even though they may need some freedom in their formative years, young kittens do, I believe, also need boundaries. They need restrictions. After all, without boundaries what joys are there in freedom? The kitten who does not know what it is *not* allowed to do will get no pleasure from doing what it *is* allowed to do. Boundaries provide security, comfort and strength and yet at the same time they also provide kittens with the sweet pleasures that come from disobedience.

Penlope allows her kittens to do very much as they please. They are allowed to scratch and claw at the furniture and at one another. They are allowed to run up and down the curtains and try out their teeth and claws on the brocade upholstery of the best dining room suite that Penelope's Uprights are so fond of. Penelope's kittens will, I fear, grow up without any of the security that is provided by firm boundaries.

Just before we left one of the kittens got lost while exploring in the garden. It took Penelope, Thomasina and I nearly three quarters of an hour to find it. I told Penelope that she really does have to give her kittens boundaries. If she insists on bringing up her family in this lackadaisical way then she is asking for trouble.

April 14th

I was terribly worried last night. I thought something dreadful had happened. The Uprights went off early in the day and by late evening still hadn't come back.

Normally when they go out and know they aren't going to get back until late they leave plenty of food out for Thomasina and myself.

45

But there was nothing!

Thomasina was in a dreadful state and I had to pretend that I wasn't worried. To try and keep her calm I said that I thought they'd probably stayed chatting with some other Uprights and I suggested that we go out and catch ourselves a couple of plump mice for our evening meal.

Thomasina couldn't concentrate but I found a pair of young fieldmice (my favourite kind) and killed them both quickly because I thought she was hungry. But Thomasina wouldn't touch hers. She was convinced that something terrible had happened.

So we both prowled around in the driveway listening for the sound of the Uprights returning.

"If they come back safely I promise that I'll always be loving and show them how much I care for them," said Thomasina. "I won't ever be sick on their bed again. And I won't use the bookcase to sharpen my claws."

By the time it was really dark we were both in quite a state. Thomasina was absolutely convinced that we would never ever see either of them again. "They've had a crash," she insisted. "And I will miss them so much. They were the kindest and sweetest Uprights any cat ever lived with. We should have shown them more affection." By this time I'd given up pretending not to be worried. I was very upset too. In my heart I thought she was right and that we would never ever see either of them again.

They got back after midnight. We heard them when they were still half a mile away. When we saw that they were both all right we were very relieved.

As soon as he got out of the car the Upright in Trousers started whistling for us. He always whistles though I don't know why he bothers. We can both recognise his footsteps a mile away. Then the Upright who wears a Skirt joined in.

Thomasina and I sat quite still in the darkness.

"I'm so glad they are safe," Thomasina said. "Come on, let's go and say 'hello'."

"I'm not going to make a fuss of them," I said.

Thomasina looked at me in amazement. She knew that moments earlier I had been distraught with worry.

"Coming in at this time of night," I said. "It's not right. They ought to have known that we'd be worried. Not to mention hungry. It's thoughtless of them."

Reluctantly, Thomasina agreed with me.

"Let's go and catch some mice," I said. "I don't want them to know that I've been hanging around here all evening waiting for them to come back home."

"OK," said Thomasina. And we both crept quietly off into the darkness leaving the two Uprights whistling and calling mournfully into the darkness.

April 17th

Today Thomasina told me that she had heard that in an average sort of year an average sort of cat will kill 50 small animals – mice, voles, shrews and suchlike. Even allowing for the number of cats who never catch anything that seems a very low estimate to me. I'm sure that Thomasina and I catch that many in a month.

Still, I've never had much faith in statistics. Ever since I was told that the average cat has 3.996 legs.

April 20th

The Upright in Trousers was sitting out in the garden today. He stayed in a deckchair for well over an hour. He pretended to be asleep but he wasn't. His eyes were half open most of the time. I wonder if Uprights are thinking about anything when they sit like that? If so,

"...in an average sort of year an average sort of cat will kill 50 small animals."

I wonder *what* they are thinking? I don't suppose I shall ever know.

April 21st

Although Penelope has become an enthusiastic hunter she realises that she will never be a great hunter. She has no real natural skill and although she has practised hard she remains too clumsy, too noisy and to undisciplined to catch anything but the slowest of small rodents. Aware of all this Penelope has started to train her kittens to hunt. Today I found her and her offspring waiting outside a shrew's hole at the bottom of their garden.

"I want my kittens to have opportunities that I never had," she explained. "I want them to be great mousers. Wouldn't it be wonderful if one of them ended up on a farm with real mousing responsibilities. Or in a hotel or restaurant kitchen."

I told her that would be nice if that was what her kittens really wanted for themselves. But I pointed out to her that she shouldn't try to make her kittens live the sort of life she might have enjoyed.

May 1st

I came back from a hunting expedition down by the river to find that the Uprights had planted a rose bush right in the middle of my main lavatory area! It is a good job that I saw it during daylight hours. At night that rose bush could have given me a very nasty surprise. I wonder how the Uprights would like it if they came home one day and found a rose bush growing out of *their* lavatory?

May 3rd

Thomasina and I were playing with a large mouse today when suddenly a huge bird swooped down out of the sky and plucked the mouse up from where it lay between us.

A bird stole our mouse!

We couldn't believe it.

"What a cheek!" said Thomasina indignantly.

"I just hope it comes back again," I said.

"I just can't get over it," said Thomasina. "A bird stealing food from us. And food that we'd caught too."

"It won't do that again," I promised. "If it comes anywhere near me again I'll show it a thing or two."

Just then there was a great fluttering sound above our heads. We both looked up and saw that the bird had indeed returned. Its huge talons were hovering just a few

"I came back from a hunting expedition to find that the Uprights had planted a rose bush right in the middle of my main lavatory area."

inches above Thomasina's head and it had the most vicious, hooked beak I have ever seen on a bird.

"It's back again," hissed Thomasina. "It's a hawk! What do you think it wants?"

"Us," I muttered under my breath.

And we scampered back through the cat flap just as fast as our legs would carry us.

"I wasn't ready for it that time," said Thomasina.

"It wasn't fair the way it just appeared out of nowhere like that," I said.

"I could see that it was worried," said Thomasina.

"It certainly didn't dare attack us," I said.

"I think it was probably terrified of us," said Thomasina.

"You're absolutely right," I said. "We showed it who's the boss."

"Serves it right for stealing our mouse," said Thomasina.

May 5th

I was in the bedroom today when I saw the Upright in Trousers at the window. He was standing on a ladder and seemed to be doing something to the window frame. Since the window was wide open I thought I'd pop out and say 'hello' to him.

I jumped up onto the window seat, onto the inside ledge and then stepped out onto the window sill.

As soon as I did I knew I'd made a mistake.

The Upright in Trousers screamed at me as loudly as he could and terrified the life out of me. He clearly didn't want my company. But worse than that was the fact that my feet felt all sticky. The window sill was covered in something horribly tacky and it covered my front paws completely. Because I never like going backwards I had to turn round before I could get back into the bedroom and to turn round I had to take my hind legs out of the window too. That meant that by the time I'd finished all four paws were covered in this horrible, white, sticky material.

Startled by all this I leapt back into the bedroom only to find that the Upright who wears a Skirt had come into the room while I'd been out on the window sill. She seemed horrified by something and chased me round and round the bedroom several times. It was terrible. Everywhere I went I could feel my paws sticking to things. They stuck to the dressing table, they stuck to the bedclothes, they stuck to the armchair in the corner of the room and they stuck to the top of the wardrobe too.

And it was there that I had to stay because the Upright who wears a Skirt had shut the bedroom door. And I

51

certainly wasn't going to try going out through the window again.

It took me nearly two hours to clean all the sticky stuff off my paws. And it tasted absolutely awful. I don't know what it was but I'm glad I'm not a window sill. I'd hate to be completely covered in the stuff.

May 6th

I consider myself a well balanced cat, able to deal with most pressure and problems. Few things really worry me. But there is one thing that really makes my back arch and my tail bristle: and that is the way that the Uprights always turn the lights off when they leave the room, even if I'm still in there.

Last night, for example, I came in rather late for supper (I'd been trying in vain to catch a vole that I felt sure I'd got cornered) and toddled into the kitchen just at the moment when the Uprights were going to bed. They both stopped for a moment to tickle me under the chin and stroke the back of my head and then they were off, leaving me in the pitch dark to try and eat my evening meal.

I know exactly why they do it, of course. It's because they think that I can see in the dark. It's true, I can see in the dark. But I can't see all *that* well, and I really do prefer to have a good, clear view of what I'm eating.

May 7th

I watched Thomasina trying to catch her first mole today. She made the mistake that we all make: she tried to pull it out of its hole by its back legs. She failed, of course, because the mole's front spade-like paws are so good at digging that it pulls itself out of reach. The only way

to catch moles is to take hold of them by their front
legs and pull them out that way.

One day I think I'll write a book and include all these
little tips and hints.

May 10th

"Don't you ever wish that you lived with an Upright?"
I asked George today.

"I have," said George. "Over the years I've lived
with several Uprights."

"Don't you like them?" I asked him.

"In many ways I'm very fond of them," said George.
"But I just don't seem to be able to live comfortably
with Uprights."

"But they can be very useful if you train them properly," I said. "Don't you think so?"

George nodded wisely. "If you can find the time and
patience to train them properly they can be a wonderful
boon to any cat," he agreed. "I remember living with
an Upright whom I thought I'd really got very well
trained. She put food down for me regularly twice a day.
All I had to do was go and sit by the empty bowl and
she'd follow, open a tin and fork out a good helping.
I managed to train her to open the door whenever I wanted
to go out. I could get her to open it and let me back
in again by jumping onto the living room window sill
and looking through the glass. That's all I had to do:
just look into the room. And she'd be up to open the
door within seconds."

"It sounds as if you were very good with Uprights,"
I told him.

"Oh, training them isn't really the problem," said
George. "It's getting them to know when to stop. *That's*
the problem. This Upright I've just been telling you about
was easy enough to train, but she was always fussing

"I could get her to open the window simply by looking through the glass," said George.

over me. Whenever I was eating she would bend down and stroke me. I hate being stroked when I'm eating. I don't know why but it just drives me mad. I'm sure she was just being loving and showing that she cared for me. But I couldn't stand it. And she was just as bad when I was trying to sleep. She couldn't leave me alone. I'd curl up on her lap for a snooze and she would just keep on stroking and tickling, stroking and tickling and tickling and stroking. There wasn't even a pattern to it, anything you could get used to. And however comfortable I am I just can't get to sleep when someone is doing all that to me.''

''Mine do that sometimes,'' I said. ''But it's just the way Uprights are, isn't it?''

''Absolutely,'' agreed George. ''I'm not suggesting that there was anything wrong with the Uprights I lived with. I'm quite prepared to admit that it was my fault. But the fact remains that I just can't live comfortably with an Upright.''

''Don't you miss having Uprights around all the time?'' I asked.

''Not really,'' said George. ''But then in some ways I've got the best of both worlds haven't I? There are lots of Uprights round here who put food out for me and give me titbits when I call by. But I don't owe them anything. I don't feel that I have to let them stroke me while I'm eating, or tickle me while I'm sleeping.''

I can understand George's point of view. But I don't think I would like his lifestyle. I rather like having one set of Uprights to look after me. All things considered we get on very well together. They get on my nerves a little sometimes. And I'm sure I'm a disappointment to them occasionally. But when you have a long term relationship with a pair of Uprights there is something special that enables you to overlook these little problems.

May 11th

Penelope came racing round this morning in a terrible state.

''Jerry Junior has disappeared,'' she cried, in great distress. ''I woke up this morning and he'd gone.''

I asked her how she knew he hadn't just wandered off and got lost in the garden.

"He's too bright to just go and get lost," she insisted. "Oh, Alice," she said. "I think he's run away."

I told her not to be so silly and promised that Thomasina and I would help her find young Jerry Junior before anything happened to him.

In order to increase our chances of success the three of us set off in different directions. Penelope headed North, Thomasina went East and I went West. We decided that it was unlikely that Jerry Junior would have gone South because that route would take him right onto the main road.

We spent the best part of the day searching for him. And in the end I found him hiding in an old garden shed at the bottom of the Cottage Hotel. He was tired, hungry and frightened.

"I sat down beside Jerry Junior and asked him to tell me what was troubling him."

"I don't want to come back," said Jerry Junior defiantly, when I asked him to follow me home.

I sat down beside him and asked him to tell me what was troubling him.

"It's the hunting," said Jerry Junior. "I'm no good

at it. And I don't think I ever will be. But Mum is so keen for me to become a great hunter. I just feel that I'm letting her down all the time. And I can't stand it any more. I think it would be better if I didn't go back.''

"Don't be silly," I told him. "Your mother loves you and misses you dreadfully. She's out searching for you now.''

"I know she loves me," said Jerry Junior. "But that just makes it worse. I just feel that I'm letting her down even more.''

"A few months ago your mother knew nothing about hunting," I told him. "It's only in the last few weeks that she's really learned the skills of hunting herself. I think she's very conscious of what she has missed and of the opportunities that have been lost to her. She wants to make sure that you don't miss out. She wants you to have the chances that she never had. She wants your life to be as exciting and as rewarding as possible.''

"I appreciate that," said Jerry Junior. "And in a way I appreciate what she's doing for me. I know she's doing it for my sake. But she expects too much. She's pushing me too hard. I realise that it will be useful if I can hunt, but there are other things I want to do. I like watching the Uprights, I like going for walks, I like smelling the flowers.''

"You also have to understand that your mother desperately wants you to be independent," I explained. "If you learn how to hunt then you can look after yourself. You won't ever need to rely on Uprights for food. Your mother has had a bit of a hard time in the last few years. Her Uprights haven't always been kind to her and I know that on several occasions she's been close to leaving them. But she's never been able to leave because she hasn't been able to hunt. She knows how frustrating that has been for her and she doesn't ever want you to be in that position. She wants you to have enough independence to be able to live your own life.''

"But she's not letting me live my own life," insisted

Jerry Junior. "She makes us all get up early in the morning and go on training runs. Then we're at it all day long and way into the night. It's all too much for me, really it is."

"Come back with me and I promise that I'll talk to your mother," I told him. "I'll try and talk some sense into her. I'll try and persuade her to let up on you."

"Would you?" asked Jerry Junior hopefully. "That would be wonderful."

"You'll still have to do some hunting practice," I told him. "I doubt if I'll be able to persuade your mother to let you give up hunting lessons completely. And even if I could I don't think I would. I also think it is important that you learn your basic hunting skills."

"If she'd just take the pressure off a little," said Jerry Junior, standing up unsteadily and moving towards me.

"I'm sure she will," I said. "It's getting late now. Let's get you back home and tomorrow morning I promise I'll have a long chat with your mother,"

Twenty five minutes later an exhausted young Jerry Junior and a tearful Penelope were cuddling and licking one another enthusiastically.

"I'm so grateful," said Penelope, lifting her head for a moment. "Really I am."

"Then you owe me a favour," I said to her.

"Anything," agreed Penelope.

"Meet me down by our greenhouse first thing tomorrow morning," I said to her. "You and I have got to have a long chat about things."

Penelope looked a little surprised, but promised to meet me as I'd asked.

May 12th

True to her promise Penelope met me by the greenhouse this morning. She was already there when I arrived just as the sun was rising.

58

"Thank you for finding Jerry Junior," said Penelope. "I don't know what I'd have done if you hadn't found him."

"Have you talked to Jerry yet?" I asked her.

Penelope shook her head. "We went straight to sleep last night. Besides, I thought you might have something you wanted to say to me before I talked to him."

"Do you know why he ran away from home?" I asked her.

Penelope shook her head.

"Are you sure you don't know?" I asked.

There was silence for a moment. "Well, I have one or two ideas," she admitted.

"Such as?"

"I've been pushing him too hard haven't I?" she said. "I was so keen for him to become a good hunter. So keen for him to become truly independent."

"He's a conscientious and loving kitten," I told her. "He desperately wants to please you. But he feels he is a failure."

"Of course he isn't a failure," interrupted Penelope.

"You know that. And I know that," I said to her. "But Jerry Junior doesn't know that. Whatever you may think about him he feels a failure. He feels that he has let you down."

"Oh dear," said Penelope, starting to cry. "I was never any good as a hunter. And now I'm no good as a mother either."

"You're a rotten hunter, but you are an absolutely smashing mother," I told her. "It's just that you've been trying a bit too hard recently. You have to give your kittens a little breathing space. You've been putting too much pressure on young Jerry Junior."

I explained to her that when cats put too much pressure on their kittens everyone feels disappointed. The kitten will be bound to rebel and the parent will be bound to feel aggrieved.

"Jerry Junior loves you a lot," I told her. "Try to

pull back a little. And try to be more patient.''

By now Penelope was sobbing her heart out. "Oh, I will Alice. Oh, I will,'' she insisted.

And then I came home for breakfast.

May 15th

The Uprights were in a terrible state today. All morning they rushed around the house as though they had only a few minutes in which to avert some dreadful tragedy. Although we are naturally calm and phlegmatic, even Thomasina and I began to feel the tension. The air was thick with it.

In the end it turned out that they were rushing simply to get things ready for a visit from other Uprights.

How silly Uprights sometimes are. I really can't see what difference all that rushing made.

May 17th

Today I broke a vase. It was a complete accident. I jumped onto the mantlepiece and the vase just fell off. I don't think I touched it at all.

But the last time I broke a vase the Upright who wears a Skirt was furious. So this time I thought I'd stay out of the way for a while. Although it rained steadily all day I didn't go back into the house until it was absolutely pitch dark and the Uprights had been calling me for several hours.

Sure enough, when I finally got back they were so pleased to see me that nothing at all was said about the vase.

Not that it was really my fault anyway.

May 18th

Tonight is the night that Oscar leaves his Upright. And we all put George's plan into action.

There were nine of us. And we started preparing for it during the afternoon. By just after midnight we were all ready, waiting in the shrubbery just outside Oscar's front door.

Thomasina had caught a fieldmouse and a shrew. Both in excellent condition. She kept the shrew in her mouth and the fieldmouse under control by repeated taps on the side of its head.

George had brought a large brown rat that was only partly subdued. Twice it tried to escape and George had to chase after it and bring it back.

Oscar himself had a large brown mouse.

Penelope had a vole that she took care not to let out of her grasp. And her kitten Jerry Junior had the tiniest of tiny shrews.

Jeremy, a ferocious tom cat that everyone except George feared, had brought a huge rabbit. But when George told him that a rat would be better he let the rabbit go, disappeared and came back less than half an hour later with the biggest brown rat I've ever seen.

Sooty and Lapsong II had both brought mice and I had a mouse too. It was quite an impressive collection of rodent wildlife.

We must have looked a strange sight as we followed Oscar around to the back of the house. There we followed silently as Oscar climbed first onto a dustbin, then onto a window ledge and finally into the kitchen through a tiny window that had been left slightly open.

''He doesn't usually leave any windows open at all at night,'' said Oscar. ''But I was sick all over the floor this afternoon and I knew he'd leave a window open to let the place air a little.''

Less than five minutes later we were all standing in the kitchen.

And then, after a nod from George, we all released our prey. For a moment or two the mice, the rats, the shrews and the vole all stood quite still, getting their bearings. It must have been quite a puzzle for them. And then one of the rats made a dash for the door which led out of the kitchen and into the hallway. Within seconds he'd disappeared. And within another twenty seconds so had all the rest of the menagerie. All in hiding.

Moving as quietly as we could we all trooped back out through the kitchen window. Poor young Jerry Junior couldn't make the jump down from the window sill to the dustbin and had to be helped by George.

Moving in single file we paraded down the garden path, over the garden gate and out into the street beyond. And there, after bidding Oscar farewell and good luck, we headed for home.

May 21st

There was nothing but those crunchy things for breakfast this morning. It seems that the Uprights forgot to buy any cans of food. Those crunchy things are all right in an emergency. But for breakfast?

In despair Thomasina and I went out hunting. She caught a mouse and I caught a shrew.

I hate shrew even more than I hate those crunchy things.

May 23rd

Sometimes I wonder what it is all about. Why are we here? What are we doing? Who put us here? And why? I wonder if other cats dwell on these things. Several times today I almost broached the subject with Thomasina. But although she is my dearest friend I didn't. I was, I supposed, worried that she might think me foolish.

May 27th

I was daydreaming on the bedroom window seat this evening when the Upright in Trousers came into the room carrying a step ladder. He put the ladder into position, climbed up it, pushed open part of the ceiling and disappeared.

At first I thought I was still dreaming. It seemed such an unlikely eventuality.

But when I jumped down from the window seat and strolled across the room I could see that there really was a step ladder standing there. And there really was a hole in the ceiling.

The temptation was irresistible. I climbed up the steps until I was on top of the step ladder and looked up through the ceiling. It was very dark and I couldn't see anything at all. Bravely, I leapt up onto the ledge that surrounded the hole.

About ten or twelve feet away I could see the Upright in Trousers moving about with a torch in his hand so I wandered over towards him. There were all sorts of interesting looking boxes strewn around.

I saw a huge cardboard box that the television set had come in and that Thomasina had played in for hours. And I spotted the two wicker baskets that the Uprights bought for us to sleep in when we were small.

I've gone over what happened next many times in my mind. But I can't think of an explanation. I had picked my way carefully across the floor between the boxes and I suddenly found myself no more than an inch or two away from the Upright in Trousers. He was sitting on his haunches holding the torch with one hand and rummaging through a small cardboard box with the other.

"The temptation was irresistible."

Not wanting to disturb him, but anxious to let him know that I was there, I reached out and rubbed my head against his thigh.

That's all I did. I just rubbed my head against his thigh.

His response was, to say the least, dramatic. He dropped the torch, screamed out loud and jumped up into the air.

Unfortunately, the ceiling just there wasn't high enough and he cracked his head against a beam. That made him scream even louder. The torch had gone out when it had fallen and so the whole area was in total darkness.

I was still wondering what had happened when the Upright in Trousers, who had been staggering about after the blow to his head, suddenly lurched to one side and disappeared up to his waist.

He screamed again, and this time I decided that it would

probably be best if I got out of his way. So I trotted over to the hole I'd jumped up through, stepped down onto the ladder and wandered back down to the bedroom.

Up above me I could still hear the Upright in Trousers screaming and shouting. And as I left the bedroom I happened to glance up and saw his slippered feet and trousered legs poking through the ceiling above me.

It was all too exciting, and since there clearly wasn't going to be any peace in the bedroom for some time I wandered out for a snooze under the willow tree.

June 3rd

I wonder why it is that Uprights always want to pick cats up?

How would they like it if huge hands came down from the sky and scooped them into the air?

They'd probably feel uncomfortable, even frightened.

Well, that's exactly how I feel.

All Uprights do it. Some, it seems to me, can hardly walk past a cat without wanting to bend down and pick it up.

Our Upright in Trousers does it all the time.

If they stopped and thought about it they would realise that if a cat really wanted to be up in their arms it would jump up there. It wouldn't wait to be picked up.

But Uprights don't always think before they act.

P.S. I've just re-read the above entry. I should perhaps explain that I am feeling rather edgy and bad tempered today. I had a thorn in my paw yesterday and it took ages to lick it out. The site still hurts a little. And then this morning an Upright came to visit and the first thing he did was pick me up. My paw landed on his shoulder with a terrible thump and the pain was still pretty terrible when I wrote that last entry.

June 10th

The Upright who smells of Jasmine came to our house today. I was delighted.

It is a long time since I last saw her. But I could remember her smell the instant she walked in through the door.

I rubbed myself round her legs to let her know that I was pleased to see her and then, as soon as she sat down, jumped onto her lap.

The one thing I have never forgotten about the Upright who smells of Jasmine is her lap. I think she has one of the most comfortable laps it has ever been my pleasure to sit upon.

I have talked at length about laps to both Thomasina and George and they both agree with me that a good lap is something very special. All Uprights have laps, of course. But it is relatively rare to find a really good, comfortable lap to sit on.

By and large we all prefer to sit on laps belonging to Uprights who wear Skirts.

It is never very fair to generalise, but on the whole I have discovered (and both Thomasina and George agree with me on this) that an Upright in Trousers tends to fidget far more than Upright who wears a Skirt. And if there is one thing that I can't stand it is a fidgety lap. There's nothing worse than settling down for a quiet, warm, comfortable snooze and then finding yourself being shaken from side to side like a tambourine.

Of course, it's not just the fidgeting that is annoying. Uprights in Trousers are also far more likely to suddenly start reading the newspaper or magazine than are Uprights who wear Skirts.

The ordinary Upright who wears a Skirt may knit or crochet a little. But she will do nothing more than give a cursory glance at a newspaper. On the other hand, an Upright in Trousers will fiddle and fidget and open and shut his newspaper with very little concern for the cat who is trying to get to sleep on his lap.

Not that fidgeting is the only difference. The lap belonging to an Upright who wears a Skirt will, generally speaking, be much softer and warmer than a lap belonging to an Upright in Trousers.

I do have to confess that my feelings about laps are coloured by the fact that a couple of years ago, when I was nothing but a kitten, I sat down on the lap of an Upright who was smoking. At the time I didn't think anything of it.

But this was destined to be a special occasion. For unbeknown to me, the smoker had let some hot ash fall onto my fur and after I had been sitting on his lap for a few moments I suddenly heard the cry "Fire!". Out of the corner of my eye I could see smoke arising from somewhere behind me. Only a few seconds later did I suddenly start to smell burning fur.

If I had been alone I wouldn't have panicked. I would have gone quietly outside, found some damp grass and rolled over and over a few times until the fire had been put out.

But the Uprights who were with me panicked.

And before I knew what was happening I was doused with a whole bucket full of water. It was a terrible experience. At the time I think I would have been happier if they'd let me burn to death. I hate water. And to have a bucket full of it thrown over you is not a pleasant feeling.

But all that was in the past.

Today I spent a very pleasant couple of hours sitting on the wonderfully soft and comfortable lap of the Upright who smells of Jasmine.

June 12th

Two strange Uprights have been staying with us for a few days. I always hate visitors. They cause so much disruption and destroy our routine. Normally the Upright in Trousers gets up at 7.30 in the morning and puts out our food before he does anything else. When there are visiting Uprights in the house he always makes them a cup of tea first. Inevitably that means that it is 8 o'clock before we're fed. And I hate having to wait for breakfast. The same thing applies in the afternoon too. The Upright who wears a Skirt normally feeds us at 5.30. But when there are strangers in the house she's always busy looking after them and Thomasina and I have to hang around the kitchen and wait until she can find a moment or two in which to open a can and fork out a plateful of nourishment.

It's not only mealtimes which get disrupted. There are a host of other annoying things too. Visiting Uprights invariably want to sit on my favourite chair. They shut doors that should be left open. And some of them have very peculiar ideas about how cats should be treated.

So, for example, one of the Uprights who has been staying this time spent hours this morning trying to teach me tricks. He had found a marble and he kept throwing it across the living room floor. It was perfectly clear that he expected me to rush after it and take it back to him, so I did it just once to make him feel good. Even though I don't like visitors very much I do feel that one has a responsibility to be sociable and welcoming.

But once wasn't enough. He kept trying the same trick time and time again, and I certainly wasn't going to waste the morning running round the living room just so that he could feel good. Once is fair enough, but what is the point of doing something time and time again?

What really made me angry was the comment he made afterwards. Our Upright in Trousers came into the room after he'd thrown the marble about a thousand times and the visitor grinned at him and said: "I've been trying to teach your cat a little trick. I thought she'd got it because she did it once, but it must have been a lucky break."

I was annoyed because the Upright clearly believed

that I wasn't intelligent enough to learn his little trick! I couldn't believe his cheek!

Uprights like that really do annoy me. They are the sort of Uprights who assume that because dogs can do tricks they are intelligent. It really is the most nonsensical argument. Dogs aren't intelligent. They are obedient. And there is a vast difference between the two. I could learn any number of tricks if I wanted to learn tricks and show off. But that's not my nature. And it's not the nature of any self respecting cat. We don't not learn tricks because we're dumber than dogs but because we're brighter than them.

Why on earth would anyone want to spend the morning racing around picking up a marble time and time again?

June 14th

It was very sunny today. I slept behind the hydrangeas.

June 16th

I wonder if I was perhaps born with less zeal that I should have. If I had to say what my favourite occupation is I would have to say sleeping. Today I woke up twice. Once for breakfast. And once for supper.

June 18th

The warmest day of the year. I spent it sitting underneath the willow tree. In the evening I discovered that an army of ants had swarmed all over me. It is going to take me days to get them all out of my fur.

June 19th

Thomasina has been helping me get rid of the ants. She says that she quite likes the taste of them. I think it must be an acquired taste.

June 20th

Twice this week the Uprights have taken mice that I have brought into the house. I don't mind this too much. We are, after all, members of the same family. But today I decided that it was about time that they learned how to catch their own mice.

To start with I needed a mouse for teaching purposes. And as always when you want one there isn't one to be seen anywhere. It took me hours to find one and when I finally did manage to corner one and bring it inside the Uprights had both gone upstairs to sleep. But some things are more important than sleep – and mouse catching is one of them.

Holding it lightly in my mouth so as not to damage it too much I took the mouse upstairs into the bedroom. There I put it down on the carpet, held it still with one paw and miaowed loudly to wake them up.

It took what seemed like a lifetime and my paw was beginning to get tired, but eventually the Upright in Trousers sat up, rubbed his eyes and switched on the bedside lamp.

I don't know why, but I hadn't expected that, and the sudden burst of light startled me so much that I lifted my paw and released the mouse.

However, I did have enough presence of mind to realise that this gave me an excellent opportunity to offer a little realistic hunting practice. So I miaowed loudly to alert the Upright and attract his attention and then I dived under the bed after the mouse.

"I eventually cornered it in an old shoe."

As soon as I got under the bed I realised that I had an enormous task in front of me. Not thinking of the difficulties they would create, the Uprights had pushed all sorts of rubbish underneath the bed. There were old cardboard boxes, blankets, shoes, a camp bed and an electric blanket. It all goes to show just how little Uprights know about mice! I couldn't see or hear the mouse anywhere. I couldn't even smell him very well because someone had kicked a tin of talcum powder under the bed and the whole area reeked of a sickly sweet perfume. I lay very still and tried to keep as quiet as possible so that I would be able to hear him moving.

But up above me the Uprights were behaving terribly. The Upright in Trousers had seen the mouse I'd brought and had woken the Upright who wears a Skirt. Both of them were so excited that they were making enough noise to make tracking an elephant impossible. The Upright in Trousers was shouting, the Upright who wears a Skirt was screaming and the bedsprings were twinging and twanging mercilessly.

I miaowed to tell them to be quiet but it didn't have any useful effect at all. Indeed, if anything, it made matters worse. So I wriggled out backwards from underneath the bed, jumped up onto the bedclothes and miaowed even more loudly at them, begging them to stop the noise they were making. Any six week old kitten would have known what I was saying.

Not my Uprights though. The Upright who wears a

Skirt scrambled up out of the bed and stood on tip toes, holding her nightdress around her body. The Upright in Trousers is usually a mite more courageous but even he seemed alarmed.

Meanwhile I had no idea where the mouse had got to and because I didn't want to lose it after having spent so long catching it in the first place I jumped off the bed and wriggled back underneath.

It took me the best part of an hour to find it. But I eventually cornered it in an old shoe. It was hiding down in the toe but I managed to hook it out with a claw without too much difficulty. Feeling quite pleased with myself I picked the mouse up in my mouth and wriggled back out from underneath the bed. Now, I thought, I'll be able to start their mouse catching lessons.

But both the Uprights had disappeared. There wasn't a sign of them in the bedroom and what was worse, the bedroom door was firmly shut. Through the thin partition wall I could hear them settling down on the spare bed.

At first I thought they had probably just got bored and given up. But on thinking about it I realised that this was almost certainly their way of letting me have the mouse for myself. They probably felt guilty for taking two mice off me already this week. Sometimes Uprights really can be thoughtful. I was quite touched and made a mental note to get them another mouse very soon.

June 23rd

Because Thomasina has worms the Uprights decided that we both must have the treatment. I don't know why they insist on treating both of us when only one of us is ill. It really doesn't make much sense to me. I have watched carefully to see if the Uprights do this to one another. And I am convinced that they do not.

As it happens it didn't matter too much because as usual I managed to avoid the medicine. I can always tell when they're going to try and give me something that will be good for me! They start by putting a large wooden tray across the cat flap. It's always the same large wooden tray and the Upright in Trousers always looks terribly pleased with himself when he's got it in position and has assured himself that I'm safely trapped in the house.

"Both the Uprights began to behave in a most alarming and unusual way."

Then the Upright who wears a Skirt starts to make a tremendous fuss of me. She picks me up, cuddles me, strokes my head, tickles me under the chin and makes those awful noises that Uprights often use when they are talking to cats, dogs and very little Uprights. While she's making a fuss of me the Upright in Trousers is busy opening a tin of my favourite food. After putting the food into a dish he then tries to break up the tablet he wants me to take and sprinkle it onto the food. This, I might point out, is the only time I get to eat by myself without having to share a dish with Thomasina!

Then, when he's finished, he'll take me from the Upright who wears a Skirt and put me down right in front of the food.

At that point both the Uprights will begin to behave in a most alarming and unusual way. The Upright who wears a Skirt will usually kneel down on the floor and sniff at the food. She'll turn, smile at me and lick her lips. She seems to be telling me how tasty the food is. But I know how tasty the food is. It's the medicine I'm worried about. The Upright in Trousers will stoop or kneel and try exactly the same thing.

To please them I'll nibble away at those lumps of food that haven't got chunks of tablet half buried in them. And to be honest it isn't at all difficult to avoid most, if not all, of the tablet. By this time the Uprights are usually so exhausted that they're happy to leave it all until tomorrow. And tomorrow is always another day.

June 28th

This morning I decided it was time I tried once again to teach the Uprights how to hunt. The last time I tried things did not go well. But it worries me sometimes that they are so incapable of catching their own food.

I spent some time looking for a suitable practice victim and eventually settled on a rather lethargic little vole. It was one of those sad little creatures that one finds from time to time. Born with no fire or purpose or ambition it made only a half hearted attempt to escape when I had it cornered. To be honest I could have caught it with my eyes shut.

When I took the vole into the living room both the Uprights were sitting down listening to the television.

The Upright who wears a Skirt was the first to see what I had in my mouth. Straight away she got over-excited. I don't know what it is about her but she gets into a terrible state whenever she sees a mouse, a shrew or a vole. I suspect that she just can't control herself when she knows that there is going to be a hunt.

She started to run around the living room making a terrible noise. The Upright in Trousers responded

"The vole didn't move. So I reached out and patted it on the head."

instantly. He jumped up and moved quickly towards me with his arms outstretched.

I have to confess that I was disappointed in both of them. The Upright who wears a Skirt is undoubtedly enthusiastic, indeed I don't think I've ever seen anyone get quite so excited by the prospect of a hunt, but she doesn't stop to think. The noise she was making would have warned every creature within a mile radius that there was something about to happen.

And the Upright in Trousers wasn't much better. You have to plan a hunt carefully and thoughtfully. Just rushing at something never works.

Actually, they could have learned a thing or two from the television. It carried on talking and ignored me completely.

I decided that if I didn't allow them to get on with it they would never learn anything, so I let the vole go and backed away from it.

What a mistake that was.

The Upright in Trousers jumped back and the Upright who wears a Skirt leapt onto the sofa. I could hardly believe my eyes. They seemed to be frightened of it. Frightened of a vole. Can you imagine that?

The vole didn't move. It stayed exactly where it was. So I patted it gently on the top of its head to remind it that even though it might have nothing to worry about from the Uprights I was still there.

That did the trick.

The vole suddenly dashed forwards, turned at a right angle and disappeared under the sofa.

The Upright who wears a Skirt didn't like that one little bit. She leapt down from the sofa, ran across the room and climbed up into one of the straight backed chairs. And the Upright in Trousers reached down into the magazine rack and picked out a newspaper which he proceeded to roll into a tight tube.

Then, while the Upright who wears a Skirt moaned and whimpered on her chair, the Upright in Trousers knelt down and poked his rolled up newspaper underneath the sofa. I wish he could have seen himself. What a silly fellow he is sometimes.

There was absolutely nothing to be done until the vole decided to pop its head out again. Hunting requires patience and cunning, thought and planning. Clumsiness and rolled up newspapers aren't likely to get you any-where.

Attempting to calm them down a little and show them just how they should do it, I strolled over to the sofa and sat down patiently to wait for the vole to emerge from its hiding place. It had to come out sometime. I knew that. And the vole knew that.

But then the Upright in Trousers did the most astonish-ing and ungrateful thing. He picked me up, carried me across the room and threw me into the kitchen.

I couldn't believe it!

I'd taken the vole into the living room purely and simply to help teach them how to hunt. And here they were refusing my help and insisting on doing it all themselves.

As the noise from the living room grew I waited with rising impatience for them to let me back into the living room again. But the door remained firmly closed.

Eventually I gave up and went back outside again. Even outside I could hear the crashing and banging of furniture as they raced around trying to catch the vole.

Sometimes I despair about Uprights.

July 4th

"If you had to choose," said Thomasina this morning, "which would you prefer: living here without the Uprights or living somewhere else with the Uprights?"

The question sent a cold chill down my spine and made my tail fur stand on end.

"What a strange question," I replied. "Why would I have to choose."

"Because," explained Thomasina, "the Uprights have been packing their belongings for three days now. I think we might be about to move."

I was so shocked that I didn't say anything.

All sorts of strange feelings and thoughts raced through my mind.

I love our home. It is full of warm spots and contains dozens of exciting nooks and crannies. And I love our garden too. Over the months I have learnt where the best mice can be found, which trees I can climb without getting stuck, where to hide to catch the juiciest spiders and where best to catch the sun.

But I am fond of our Uprights too. I know that they are only Uprights but I've grown very attached to them. Sometimes they can be a little annoying but they are kindly creatures. They mean well and I know that they always have our best interests at heart.

"I'd go with the Uprights," I said at last.

"Me too," said Thomasina. "But I hope they take the bed with them. It's very comfortable. And I'd miss the greenhouse. And I hope we don't move before I've caught that shrew I spotted in the rockery the other day!"

July 5th

Since Thomasina mentioned it to me it has become increasingly clear that the date of our move cannot be far away. The Uprights spent nearly all day filling suitcases. And there were clothes strewn all over the bedroom for hours.

I can't understand why the Uprights have so many belongings. The Upright who wears a Skirt must have dozens of different outfits and the Upright in Trousers is just as bad. Not that it's just clothes that they seem to collect. There are thousands of books scattered around the house and in the kitchen there are cupboards full of cups and plates and knives and forks. They hardly ever have more than two or perhaps four visitors and yet they have enough crockery to cope with an invading army of thousands.

Why do they need all these things? What are they for, I wonder?

July 6th

The Little Upright who lives next door had a birthday party today. There were games out on the lawn and huge quantities of sandwiches, jellies and fizzy drinks were consumed.

If I had to be an Upright I would choose to be one of the Little variety, I think.

The Bigger Uprights seem to have far less fun. They are always busy doing chores and are for ever conscious of their responsibilities.

Thomasina says that the Little Uprights eventually grow up into Large Uprights. I find that difficult to believe. All other creatures become wiser and more independent as they grow older. Why should Uprights be so very different?

July 7th

Thomasina woke me this morning by hitting me sharply on the side of my face.

"What's the matter?" I demanded sleepily.

"They're leaving," said Thomasina, with a touch of desperation in her voice. "The Uprights. They're going."

I still didn't understand what she meant.

"The Uprights are moving house," said Thomasina, licking my face to help me wake up faster.

Hardly believing what I was hearing I followed her out of the bedroom and down the stairs.

She was absolutely right. The Uprights were standing outside putting their suitcases into the back of their motor car.

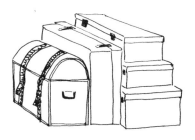

"I slowly realised what was happening. They were going to leave us."

My first thought was that it was a good job that Thomasina had woken me, because if she hadn't we would almost certainly have missed the move completely and been left behind by ourselves.

I ran up to the Upright in Trousers and brushed against his legs to remind him that I was there. Thomasina rubbed against the legs of the Upright who wears a Skirt.

She bent down and stroked Thomasina's head. And then with a sad look in her eyes she climbed into the motor car. The Upright in Trousers tickled me under the chin and then he too disappeared into the motor car.

79

It was only then that I slowly realised what was happening. They were going to leave us.

Thomasina and I had decided that we wanted to move with them. We'd never imagined that the Uprights would decide to move without us.

July 8th

The Uprights Thomasina and I had grown accustomed to think of as *our* Uprights had only been gone for a few hours when the new Uprights arrived.

We recognised them immediately. Both of them have been frequent visitors before but we'd always thought that it was because they were friends of our Uprights. We never thought they were planning to move in.

Since they arrived they have been very good to us, giving us fresh cream and all sorts of other delicacies. But Thomasina and I still find it difficult to believe that our Uprights should leave us with the house, passing us on to the next occupants like the curtains and the carpets.

July 10th

I caught a shrew. Thomasina caught a vole.

July 16th

I caught a vole. Thomasina caught nothing.

July 19th

Neither Thomasina nor I caught anything today. It rained a lot in the afternoon.

July 21st

I was sitting underneath the willow tree this afternoon when I heard something I thought I'd never hear again.

First, I heard a motor car arriving and then I heard footsteps that I recognised instantly. The Upright in Trousers and the Upright who wears a Skirt were back!

I raced up the garden, across the patio and into the front drive. And there they were! They looked a little browner than they had been when they'd left us. But they had all their bags with them.

I couldn't believe my ears or my eyes. And nor could Thomasina when she turned up on the scene a few moments later.

It was a joyful reunion. Thomasina and I both forgot the feelings of disappointment that we'd endured. Our Uprights were back. That was all that mattered.

I feel very happy tonight. I shall sleep well.

July 23rd

Penelope came round today in quite a state. She has suddenly decided that she doesn't like her shape.

"I'm far too fat," she moaned. "I put on a lot of weight when I was expecting the kittens. And I've never got my old figure back again."

I told her that I thought she had a wonderful figure and that she should stop torturing herself.

I honestly don't think I've ever met a cat who has

been entirely satisfied with her body. There is, it seems, always something that isn't quite right, something that spoils the overall effect and something that needs a little attention.

Cats who are long-haired always seem to want to have shorter hair. They talk enviously of the advantages of having short hair. And they moan endlessly abut the problems of hair balls and staying cool in summer.

On the other hand, cats who are short-haired admire their long-haired friends. They talk about them with ill disguised envy.

Cats with small snub noses always seem to want longer, sharper featured noses. Cats with sharp featured noses always want snub noses. Cats who are petite always want to be larger while cats who look like rolled up hearth rugs always want to be slight and slender. And all cats worry about their markings. A ginger cat would really prefer to be a mackerel tabby. A Siamese would prefer to be a jet black alley cat. And so on. Dissatisfaction, envy and jealousy are, it sometimes seems to me, normal feline occupations.

What we all tend to forget is that although the grass may seem greener in another field there are *always* weeds and cowpats and rabbit holes to contend with. The cat with a coat that would look skimpy on a peach sees only the obvious advantages of having a thick fur coat. She doesn't see the discomfort that can accompany such a wealth of fur.

The truth is that fur deep beauty is fragile. You could have the most perfect bone structure, the most luxuriant fur, the most captivating eyes and the most even whiskers and yet wander through life without causing more than a temporary ripple of envy and natural curiosity. For it is not appearance that makes a cat attractive, exciting, devastating and irresistible. It is the sparkle in her eyes, the softness and affection in her purr and the feeling that she cares and is interested that makes the most lasting and significant impression on everyone around.

Minor physical imperfections really do not matter. Truly magical beauty has nothing to do with a perfect nose or intriguing markings. Beauty is there inside each and every one of us. You only have to believe it for it to be visible.

I tried to explain all this to Penelope. But I do not think that she was convinced.

July 25th

Thomasina and I had a little fun with a visiting Upright this afternoon.

As soon as she arrived it was fairly clear that she didn't like us. So when she sat down we both made a tremendous fuss of her. Thomasina jumped up onto her lap and I lay down between her feet. She didn't even dare touch Thomasina who had a wonderfully peaceful time on her lap. (Which she later said was quite as warm and comfortable as any lap she's ever lain on.)

Eventually the Upright in Trousers took pity on the visitor and moved both Thomasina and I away from her.

But from the twinkle that was in his eye I can tell that even he thought it rather an amusing incident.

July 29th

A huge ginger tom that I've never seen before wandered into our garden today. He spent some time lying underneath the hydrangeas and using our trees to sharpen his claws. But neither Thomasina or I dared say anything to him. He looked most ferocious.

As the ginger tom left the garden Thomasina made a number of rather rude remarks about his colouring.

"It was fairly clear that she didn't like us. So we made a tremendous fuss of her."

I told her that was unfair and that her behaviour was racist.

August 3rd

I spent most of today sitting on a wall watching dogs. I made four observations.

First, dogs are totally dependent on Uprights. The dog at the house next door cannot even go for a walk by itself! When it goes for a walk it has to be connected to its Upright by a lead!

Second, they have absolutely no pride. The dog at the house next door has learnt all sorts of pitiful tricks. To earn a biscuit he will roll over on his back, put all four paws into the air and pretend to die. To get a pat of encouragement he will sit up on his hind legs and beg. It is sad to see a grown animal debase itself so.

Third, they have no sense of hygiene. Dogs have to be washed and their toilet habits leave a lot to be desired.

Fourth, they are stupid. Today I watched a dog burying a bone in a nearby garden. What possible purpose can there be to this bizarre act? If the bone is worth eating then it should be enjoyed, not buried.

After considerable thought I have come to the conclusion that dogs are the dumbest of animals.

August 5th

I really do hate making decisions. Life is so full of them. This evening I was fed up, and I told Thomasina how I felt.

"There are always choices to be made," I complained. "Whether to eat the meat that has been put out or to try the new crunchy things they've bought. Whether to go out mouse hunting or shrew hunting. Whether to sharpen my claws on the oak tree or the sycamore tree. And so on. Decisions. Decisions. Decisions."

"You need to rest and relax," said Thomasina.

"How?" I demanded.

"Go and lie down somewhere," said Thomasina.

"Where?" I asked.

"Underneath the willow tree," she replied. "Or on the window seat. On the sofa. Or underneath the garden bench."

Dear old Thomasina. She means well.

August 9th

A most embarrassing incident occurred this morning. Normally I can tell who is coming down the path to the house by listening to their footsteps.

My Upright in Trousers has a long stride and a thumping footfall. My Upright who wears a Skirt has a much shorter stride and a clicking footfall. He walks slowly. She walks slightly faster if she is alone and much faster if she is with him.

"Normally I can tell who is coming to the house by listening to their footsteps."

The Little Upright who delivers the morning newspaper has a half skipping, half scampering gait and always wears rubber-soled training shoes. The Upright who comes once every three months to look at the electricity meter has a very slow, very leisured tread, huge solid boots and an inability to lift his left heel completely off the ground. And the Upright who brings the morning mail walks evenly on boots with nails in them and moves very quickly indeed.

Of all the Uprights who visit our home regularly the one I like best is the one who delivers the mail. He always stops to say ''hello'' and to show a little affection. So many Uprights are for ever in a hurry. But even though his walking pace is hurried he manages to find the time to stroke my back and tickle me under the chin. I usually make sure that I'm around when he calls so that we can pay our respects to one another.

This morning I was in the garden sunning myself when I heard the garden gate swing open. It was the time when the Upright delivering the mail usually arrives and it sounded just like his footsteps.

So, naturally, I stood up, stretched and wandered over to greet him.

It was only when I was already twining in between his legs and rubbing my chin against his ankle that I suddenly realised that it wasn't the same Upright.

It was an entirely different Upright. This one smelt quite differently and made a different noise when he sorted through the letters in his bag. I had approached and shown affection to a complete stranger.

I was mortified. I ran off quickly, of course. But I was deeply embarrassed. I'm glad no one else was around to see me make such a fool of myself.

August 12th

Thomasina's favourite game is to leap on my back when I am least expecting an attack. She seems to think this is terribly funny. This morning she leapt on me no less than six times. Twice she ambushed me while I was walking down the garden path and on the other occasions she managed to ambush me inside the house.

But I got my own back this afternoon.

I waited until she'd dug herself a nice large, round hole in the garden, and then I jumped.

I wish I could have recorded the look on her face.

August 15th

I very nearly caught my first starling today.

It was sitting on a branch no more than ten or twelve feet above me. Keeping my eye on it as well as I could I stalked around the back of the tree and stealthily climbed up the bark until I reached a lower branch. There I sat for a moment watching it. I felt sure that it hadn't seen me. Instead of watching out for possible predators it was making a terrible noise.

I then carefully and slowly crept upwards until I was on a higher branch. I was now level with the starling. I had to move very carefully because birds can swivel their eyes round and see through a full circle if they want to.

The starling didn't seem to have seen me and so I cautiously crept around the trunk of the tree and onto the branch where it was sitting. Keeping low and crawling as slowly as I possibly could I gradually got closer and closer until eventually I was no more than two feet from it. Gingerly I stood up and prepared to launch myself at the bird. I knew that I'd probably fall to the ground but I thought that with a little luck I could probably keep hold of the starling.

I got myself comfortable, tensed my back legs and prepared to pounce. I could almost feel the bird in my grasp.

And then it flew away.

"I very nearly caught my first starling."

I do think that it is unfair when birds do that. How are cats expected to catch them when they can suddenly fly away? It's cheating.

Actually I wasn't all that disappointed. Birds are all bone and feather. They have hardly any meat on them and they don't taste all that good. That's what I've heard anyway.

August 17th

"Look at all these loose hairs on this chair," I heard the Upright who wears a Skirt say this afternoon. "Alice must be moulting."

I brushed every single one of those hairs out of my coat with my tongue. I really do object to the implication that they have fallen out.

August 20th

I have five favourite sleeping spots and three of them were out of action today.

My fifth favourite sleeping place is outside, down at the bottom of the garden underneath the willow tree. It is an excellent place to curl up when the sun is shining and the weather is particularly hot. The ground underneath the willow tree is always soft and the grass around the base of the trunk is long and exceptionally cool.

My fourth favourite spot is in the spare bedroom on top of the wardrobe. It's a difficult place to get to and Thomasina can't manage it. That's really why I like it. If she's being a nuisance or if we've had a row I always go up there for a nice, quiet, peaceful snooze.

My third favourite place is on the window seat in the Upright's bedroom. I used to like sleeping on their bed but Thomasina took over that position so now I usually sleep on the window seat during the night and, indeed, during the daytime if it is raining or particularly cold. There is a radiator not far away and the window seat is always really cosy. (We do sleep together very occasionally but Thomasina dreams an awful lot and twitches a good deal. I prefer to sleep by myself.)

My second favourite sleeping place is outside underneath the garden bench. The lawn mower doesn't get under there and so the grass is always fairly long. Over the months I have managed to flatten it down quite a lot. Long grass that has been flattened makes a wonderfully soft cushion. I usually sleep there if it is really hot or if it is warm but drizzling. It is cosy and very sheltered.

My very favourite sleeping spot is on top of the low wall that surrounds the herb garden. The wall is about three feet high and gives me a wonderful view of most of the garden. It means that I can watch mice, birds and butterflies all from the same position. But the real advantage of it is that it gets the sun for most of the day. And because it is sheltered rather well there is hardly ever any wind. It's a perfect size for sleeping too – there is plenty of room to stretch out and really relax.

Three out of those five sleeping places were completely

"Someone had put a suitcase on top of the wardrobe and there was no room left for me."

91

out of action for the whole day.

I discovered the first problem just after breakfast when I went upstairs to escape Thomasina who was behaving abominably. Someone had put a suitcase on top of the wardrobe and there was no room left for me. The suitcase was right in the middle, leaving only a thin border of space around it. There certainly wasn't enough room for me to lie down and relax. And I couldn't lie down on top of the suitcase because there was only about three inches between it and the ceiling.

So, unable to sleep on top of the wardrobe, I went down to the garden to sleep under the willow tree. That too was impossible. The whole area was crawling with ants. Thousands of them. I hate ants. They itch and they itch and they itch and it takes hours to find them all once they've got into your fur. I certainly wasn't going to lie down there while they were crawling all over the place.

Because it was rather overcast and certainly not warm enough for gentle sunbathing, my next stop was the garden bench. But that was out of action too. The Upright in Trousers was on his hands and knees cutting the long grass with a pair of big scissors. It took me months to flatten that grass and turn it into a really comfortable cushion.

In the end I gave up and went indoors and settled down on the window seat. But I have to say that I sometimes wonder what is happening to the world.

August 25th

Late this afternoon I saw a squirrel sitting on the lawn looking as if it owned the place. I was furious. Squirrels are among the most possessive of all rodents and they know very well that they are supposed to keep to their own territories. If Thomasina and I had dared to venture onto his favourite tree he would have gone beserk. But the trouble with squirrels is that they tend to forget that they are nothing more than rats with bushy tails. They get so much attention from Uprights that they think they're something very special. It goes to their heads and they think they can do whatever they like.

Full of anger I decided to chase the squirrel away. I chased it across the lawn, through the rhododendron bushes, round the base of the sycamore tree, up the laburnum tree and across into the large oak tree that stands at the far corner of the garden.

Normally I take great care with that particular tree. I've been up it many times in the past and from bitter experience I know that it is easier to climb up it than it is to climb down again. There is a particularly tricky stretch about twelve feet up in the air where coming down can be a real nightmare.

But chasing after that squirrel I completely forgot about the problem of coming back down again. I just raced up the tree and then watched, half satisfied but half frustrated as it leapt from the oak tree across to a nearby silver birch.

After staying where I was for a few moments to make sure that the cheeky creature didn't come back again I started to make my way back down.

And that was the point at which it all became rather tricky. And I found myself temporarily marooned up in the tree. Naturally, I miaowed a little to let Thomasina and the Uprights know where I was. I didn't want them to start worrying if I was late getting back for supper.

Then, before I knew what was happening, the Upright in Trousers appeared with a ladder. He obviously thought I was stuck and needed help. I was moritified. Me, stuck up a tree! I tried to make it clear that I didn't need his help but he wouldn't listen. Before I could do anything about it he'd climbed up the ladder, scooped me into his arms and carried me back down to earth. I struggled as much as I could just to let anyone who was watching see that I really didn't want to be carried down, and about four feet from the bottom of the ladder I leapt out of his arms onto the grass.

Thomasina teased me mercilessly, of course. I tried to explain to her that I hadn't been stuck at all, but I honestly don't think that she believed me.

Finally, just to round off the day, when I followed them all back into the kitchen I couldn't help noticing that the squirrel was sitting on the lawn again.

August 28th

A terrible thing happened to Thomasina this morning. I was sitting in the living room having a snooze when she came in and jumped up onto the top of the record player.

Unfortunately for Thomasina, the record player was switched on and the lid had been left up. The result was that Thomasina landed on a long playing record that was going round and round at 33 revolutions a minute.

I wish I could have captured the look on her face as she whirled round and round. The noise was awesome. The needle got pulled across the record and Thomasina herself miaowed loud and long in surprise and distress.

She was so startled by this strange event that it took her some time to realise exactly what had happened. And when she tried to jump off she found that she couldn't. Every time she pressed down with her back legs to leap down onto the floor the record whirled round a little faster and she stayed exactly where she was.

Poor Thomasina. It gave her quite a fright.

August 30th

I met Marmalade this morning. I quickly discovered that Marmalade is probably the most stupid cat in the whole world.

"Anything exciting happening?" I asked him as we both watched a cabbage white butterfly dancing just above our heads.

"My Uprights are a bit miserable so I came out for a stroll," said Marmalade.

I asked him why.

"I think I'll have that butterfly," said Marmalade. "Do you mind?"

"No. You go ahead," I said generously.

"They're burying the guinea pig," said Marmalade. "That's why they're all so miserable. Though I can't understand why any of them should get upset over a guinea pig."

"What was wrong with him?" I asked.

Marmalade looked at me with puzzlement in his eyes. "He was dead," he explained. "They were burying him because he was dead."

And as he spoke he launched himself into the air, caught the cabbage white butterfly in his jaws, crunched it and then swallowed it.

I sometimes wonder how it is that a cat who is so stupid is able to catch butterflies with such graceful ease. It is perhaps God's way of sharing out his gifts to us.

September 1st

I went up the stairs last night and had a terrible shock. The Upright who wears a Skirt was in bed by herself. There was no sign at all of the Upright in Trousers.

I've never known him to be out alone at night before. And it worried me.

All sorts of things went through my mind.

Had he been injured by a car?

Had he been attacked and killed by other Uprights?

Had he lost the scent and been unable to find his way back home?

"Marmalade launched himself into the air and caught the butterfly."

Or had he decided that he didn't want to live with the three of us any more?

I was very frightened.

I jumped up onto the bed where Thomasina was already curled up on top of the bedclothes, tucked in beside the

Upright who wears a Skirt. I stepped round her and went right up close to the sleeping Upright. Her face seemed calm and unworried.

Tentatively, I reached forward and nudged her face. She opened one eye, smiled at me and pulled a hand out from underneath the bedclothes. Then she reached out and stroked my head.

I knew then that everything was all right.

And so I curled up beside her face and tried to get to sleep.

But I have to confess that I slept only fitfully.

September 2nd

I spent all morning waiting by the front gate, hoping every minute to hear the Upright in Trousers' footsteps on the path.

He finally arrived back in the early afternoon. He was carrying a large bag and he looked very tired. But when I rushed up to him and gave a short greeting miaow he bent down and picked me up.

I was so delighted to see him that I didn't mind at all.

September 4th

I went out early this morning for a stroll round the garden and when I got back for breakfast I discovered that the Uprights had filled our food dish with a completely new type of food.

Thomasina was sniffing at it and tasting it in a most suspicious manner. I was surprised by this because Thomasina will normally eat anything that keeps still.

"It's horrid," she told me as I settled down beside her. "It's not the sort we usually have."

Cautiously I poked out my tongue and took a taste. It was appalling. I wouldn't have given it to a dog. And you know how I feel about dogs.

Just then the Upright who wears a Skirt bent down over us and started to caress our necks. She never normally does that. Not while we're eating. So I guessed that something was wrong.

"It's cheap stuff," I said to Thomasina, jerking my head away from the food bowl. "Don't eat it."

Thomasina looked across at me, clearly puzzled.

"It's a tin of cheap food," I explained. "They're trying it out on us. To see if we'll eat it."

"I discovered that the Uprights had filled our food dish with a completely new type of food."

"I don't like it," said Thomasina. "I prefer the stuff we always used to have."

"Come on," I said to Thomasina. "Let's go."

And with that we both turned away from our breakfast and went outside.

"What are we going to do now," asked Thomasina. "I'm absolutely starving."

"We're going to catch our own breakfast," I said.

Thomasina looked surprised. "Hunting for food is all right when you've had a good meal," she said. "But I'm too hungry to go hunting."

"Do you want to eat that rubbish for the rest of your life?" I asked her.

She grimaced and shook her head. "Of course I don't," she said emphatically.

"Then follow me," I told her.

It took us the best part of an hour and a half to catch anything. And then it was a tiny shrew with hardly any meat on it at all.

"I hate shrews," Thomasina complained. "They taste all bitter. I never eat shrews."

But she ate her half when I pointed out that it was that or nothing.

"Can't we go back and wait for them to put something else down?" asked Thomasina.

Sometimes she is so naive. She just doesn't understand Uprights very well at all.

"They must have bought that food cheap," I reminded her. "And for all we know they might have bought a whole case. Persuading them that we aren't going to eat it isn't going to be easy."

"So what do we do?" asked Thomasina.

"We stay out all day," I said to her. "And we don't go back until very late tonight."

"Oh, I can't," said Thomasina.

But she did.

We had a bit of luck a couple of hours later and caught two large really fleshy mice at the back of a greenhouse belonging to a neighbouring Upright. With full stomachs we carried on hunting with renewed enthusiasm.

It's a funny thing about hunting. When you're really

hungry you don't have the energy to catch anything. But when you're feeling comfortably full you have all the energy you need.

During the day we managed to catch and eat quite an assortment of wildlife. In addition to the mice and the shrew we found quite a lot of spiders and flies and Thomasina even managed to catch a couple of butterflies. Butterflies aren't very filling but I'm told that they taste wonderful.

We stayed out of the house until it was dark.

Twice when it rained I was very tempted to give in and go back. I kept thinking of my comfortable window seat. But in situations like this one has to be strong. And I knew that Thomasina wouldn't have the strength of mind to fight temptation. So I said nothing.

And then we heard the Uprights calling for us.

Thomasina turned towards the house immediately.

"Where are you going?" I demanded.

"Back home," said Thomasina. "They're calling. They'll be worried. Besides, they've probably put some new food out for us."

"Stay here," I ordered.

She looked puzzled.

"We're going to stay out for another hour at least," I told her. "We want to be absolutely sure that when we go back that cheap food has disappeared for good. And while we're at it we might as well take the opportunity to teach them a lesson. I don't want to have to go through this again, do you?"

Thomasina saw the sense of what I was saying.

And so we crouched in the dark at the bottom of the garden for well over an hour. Several times we heard both the Uprights come out into the garden and call for us. The Upright in Trousers walked right past us a couple of times as he searched for us among the undergrowth. And we could hear the Upright who wears a Skirt calling for us with desperation in her voice. It was very difficult to ignore their calls. But for their sake as well as our

100

own we knew that we had to wait until the message had been well and truly rubbed in. If there was one thing that I've learned over the years it is that Uprights tend to have very short memories.

When we finally did go back to the house the Uprights were sitting down in the kitchen having a cup of tea. They were silent and glum but as we climbed slowly and weakly through the cat flap they rushed towards us with arms outstretched.

I had warned Thomasina that she had to look tired and hungry and she did a wonderful job. Even I felt sorry for her.

Within seconds we were carried across the kitchen to our bowls. There was a dish full of corned beef and another filled with creamy milk. Better than I'd hoped for. And there was absolutely no sign at all of the horrid, cheap food that had been there at breakfast time.

The Uprights made such a fuss of us and treated us so well that I decided that we'd have to disappear for a day rather more often.

September 7th

Lapsong II came round this morning to show us her latest collar. She claims that it is studded with diamonds and plated with 9 carat gold.

Thomasina was quite envious.

But later I explained to her that collars can be very dangerous for cats. ''I once heard about a cat who strangled herself when her collar caught in a tree branch,'' I told her. I also pointed out that gold plating is very unsatisfactory. It can irritate the skin quite dreadfully.

September 12th

Lapsong II has a habit of ''labelling'' every cat she meets or talks about. Today, for example, she was talking to me about Marmalade (with whom she had struck up a most unlikely friendship) and every time she referred to him she insisted on calling him "Marmalade the TV cat".

(I happen to know that Marmalade isn't a TV cat at all. He went for a cat food audition but never got the job.)

And during the space of fifteen minutes she also talked to me about Blackie the Mouser (a friend of hers whom I have never met but who is renowned for his skills in catching mice) and Harriet the Tail (a rather unfortunate mixed tabby who lost half her tail in a clash with a bicycle).

After she'd gone I thought about this strange habit of hers. And eventually I realised that there is, in fact, nothing particularly unusual in what she does. It is true that Lapsong II seems to have taken the whole thing to new heights of perfection, but this trick of labelling one another is something that we all tend to do quite frequently.

We don't just base our labels on skills or achievements, of course. We tend to pick out anything that seems unusual or dramatic and use that as a label. So, for example, we think of Konig III as the Millionaire's Cat, and Carla as the Stray, even though she's been with the Uprights in Tennyson Avenue for two years now.

If we only used these labels as signposts or pointers to help us identify particular individuals in our minds all would be fine. But we don't. Too often we label each other according to some personal whim or passing fancy and then assume that everyone will behave according to the labels we've chosen.

We have our own built-in theories about what Pedigree Cats are like, and so when we meet someone labelled "Pedigree Cat" we think we know what he is going to be like. We know what Strays are supposed to be like, and so when we meet someone labelled '"Stray" we think we know all we need to know about them.

Our attempts to label cats lead us into all sorts of deadly traps. We make assumptions about other cats which lead to misunderstandings and unhappiness. And other cats make assumptions about us which lead to all sorts of agonies and despair. Labels make us shy away from other cats who might have fascinated us and we allow our prejudices to imbue each label with significance it does not merit.

The world in which we live is endlessly confusing. But by labelling one another we do not detract from that confusion. We add to it. Each one of us is different at each moment. And each one of us is different in each others eyes. It is those differences which make us so fascinating. It seems an awful pity to try to erase those variations by searching for small, neat labels with which to typecast one another.

I think that it is important to remember that one cat's niece could be another cat's aunty.

September 15th

Thomasina had a hairball today and vomited all over the sofa. The Uprights were surprisingly sympathetic. The Upright in Trousers cleaned up the mess with a cloth and some foul smelling fluid while the Upright who wears a Skirt cuddled and comforted Thomasina and told her that she wasn't to worry about it in the slightest.

Aren't Uprights wonderfully kind?

September 16th

Thomasina and I were sitting in the sun today when she turned to me and asked me a question that had clearly been weighing heavily on her mind for some time.

103

"Alice," she said, "what is the purpose of those Uprights who don't live with cats?"

I thought about it for a quarter of an hour before replying. I examined every explanation I could think of. I tried to be logical, fair and objective.

"I don't know," I said eventually.

Setpember 19th

A strange thing occurred to me today.

How do they get cat food into cat food tins?

The tins are sealed and have to be opened with a special cutting device.

I can't believe that Uprights are clever enough to get cat food inside one of those sealed tins. And wrapping a can around a block of food is also clearly impossible.

So how do they do it?

Do they perhaps grow the tins somewhere with the cat food inside them? Is there, I wonder, a special catfood tree somewhere? And are the tins just thick skins? Like orange peel or banana skins?

There are so many imponderables. And so many questions to which even I do not know the answers.

September 20th

The Upright in Trousers caught me out today.

My excuse is that there were several Uprights visiting the house and I was feeling very stressed. As I've explained before I really do hate having lots of visitors.

Anyway, I was sitting underneath the dining room table well out of range, when suddenly the Upright in Trousers

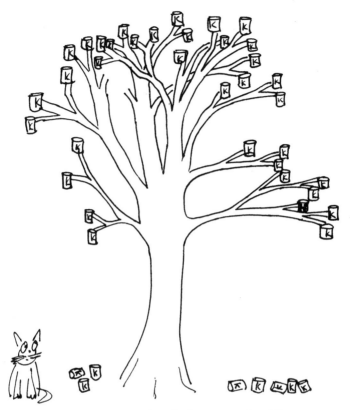

"Is there a special cat food tree somewhere?"

came over and dropped a table tennis ball right in front of me.

Naturally, I knocked it back towards him. It was a reflex action. It just seemed a perfectly natural thing to do.

Then he dropped the ball again.

And without thinking I knocked the ball straight back to him once more.

105

"Without thinking I knocked the ball straight back to him once more."

I know it is difficult to believe this but at the time I just honestly thought that he was being clumsy.

Then I heard him tell the visiting Uprights how clever I was. He turned to me with a big grin on his face and tickled me under the chin.

I was absolutely furious. I suddenly realised that he had used me and tricked me. I desperately hoped that he would drop the ball a third time. I was all prepared to ignore him. But he wasn't going to push his luck. He just put the ball back into his pocket and disappeared into the kitchen.

I was seething.

About a minute later he returned from the kitchen clutching a bowl of cold custard.

Instantly I knew what was going on. This was his way of saying ''sorry'' for having used me in such a despicable manner and for having made me look such a fool.

Well, I wasn't going to let him get away with it. Very slowly I stood up, arched my back and stretched my legs. Then I walked very slowly over to the dish he was holding, lowered my nose and sniffed. Then, summoning up every ounce of determination I could find, I walked straight past the bowl and through the cat flap out into the garden.

I hated doing it, but he had to be taught a lesson. I wasn't going to forgive him that easily.

I do have to confess that I had thought that after a few hours I'd be able to creep back into the house and enjoy my cold custard anyway. But it didn't work out quite that well. While I was out Thomasina cleaned the bowl completely.

All things considered today was not a good day.

September 24th

Lapsong II graced us with another visit this afternoon. She wanted to tell us that her Upright has bought her a new basket to sleep in. Neither Thomasina nor I could share her enthusiasm. Our Uprights bought us wicker baskets once when we were small. We slept in them for a couple of nights, but only because we didn't want to hurt the Uprights' feelings. After that we hardly ever went into them. Even with a rug in it a wicker basket can never be as comfortable as an interior sprung mattress or a sofa cushion.

''Mine has my name on it,'' Lapsong II told us with

undisguised pride. "And it was made by an artist working in the Cotswolds."

"Very nice," said Thomasina.

"It's painted with a high gloss varnish."

"Splendid," I nodded approvingly.

"There's a new plaid rug in the bottom of it," Lapsong II went on.

"Lovely," murmured Thomasina. She yawned politely.

"And it has handles on each side of it."

We both said how convenient that was.

Lapsong II looked disappointed. She had clearly expected us to be more impressed.

"Well, I have to be going," she said, lifting her head so that we had a good view of her jewel encrusted genuine leather collar. "My Upright will worry about where I've got to." She waited a moment. "It's the collar you know," she said. "It's rather valuable."

"Of course," yawned Thomasina. Sometimes I think she over does it to the point of being downright rude.

"And besides," said Lapsong II, turning to leave, "the Upright has got me a salmon steak for tea."

And with that final thrust she put her tail into the air and flounced away.

"Poor old Lapsong II," said Thomasina when she was out of earshot. "She does try so hard."

And then we both burst into a fit of the giggles.

Actually, both Thomasina and I feel dreadfully sorry for poor Lapsong II. She is so anxious to gather new possessions and enhance her status with belongings that she has very little free time in which to enjoy herself.

And she is always under so much self imposed pressure. When Penelope was given a collection of felt mice for Christmas Lapsong II sulked for nearly a fortnight. Her Upright had bought her a pot of cat nip, a new travelling basket, antique porcelain foodbowls and a piece of salmon. But she hadn't got a family of felt mice. And she was consumed with jealousy.

108

Thomasina and I have talked about this at some length and have come to the conclusion that Lapsong II gets her wants and needs mixed up. She puts herself under a tremendous amount of pressure to acquire things. She is constantly aggrieved and rarely enjoys herself even though her Upright adores her and spoils her dreadfully.

It really does all come down to wants and needs. She wants something, thinks she needs it and then gets upset if she doesn't have it.

I do think it's sad.

September 29th

I've got another tick. This one is round the back of my ear and it is desperately annoying.

Why, I wonder, do ticks always manage to end up in the most uncomfortable places?

October 1st

When I woke up this morning the tick behind my ear had gone.

Good riddance.

October 4th

I'm going to leave. The Uprights really have gone too far and I am going to leave them to cope by themselves.

This afternoon I came into the kitchen feeling really hungry and found that they'd forgotten to put any fresh crunchy things down for me. There was absolutely nothing at all to eat.

I was about to give up and go out and catch the mouse that lives down by the garden bench (it's a really stupid mouse that I've been keeping for a day when I really want to boost my confidence by catching a "dead cert") when I suddenly realised that there was something up on the kitchen table that smelt very good.

"I found a whole raw chicken. It smelt and looked marvellous."

Now I know that they don't really like me jumping up onto the kitchen table but there was no one around and I didn't think it could possibly do any harm just to have a look and see what was smelling so good.

So up I leapt.

And there on a dish I found a whole raw chicken. It smelt and looked absolutely marvellous. It was perfectly clear that there was more than enough meat for all of us. And so I succumbed to temptation and tasted it. Nothing more than a taste. A mouthful from one wing, and perhaps two delicious mouthfuls from the breast.

I was having trouble with the skin which was unusually tough and so I didn't hear the Upright who wears a Skirt come into the room.

She hit me.

She actually hit me.

I've never known either of them do that before and I was staggered. It wasn't so much the blow that I received (to be perfectly honest it was a glancing blow and didn't hurt me at all) as the fact that she actually wanted to hit me.

I must have stood for a moment quite bewildered. And then when I saw the look of genuine anger on her face I ran off outside.

I was devastated. And very confused.

All I'd done had been to take a couple of bites out of a huge chicken. And there was plenty for all of us and I'm always prepared to share my food with Uprights. I can't count the number of shrew, voles, moles and mice I've left out for them as presents. She ought to know that I wouldn't dream of eating any of it if I hadn't been hungry. And it wasn't as if I'd eaten it all. Just a couple of mouthfuls. That's all I'd had.

I was really hurt by it all. Deeply offended. And I really am thinking of leaving.

October 5th

I am very puzzled today.

Yesterday I took a couple of bites out of a chicken that was sitting on a plate on the kitchen table. The Upright who wears a Skirt was furious and hit me.

And this morning I found that the whole chicken had been thrown into the dustbin. Not just the carcase. But the whole uncooked chicken. Thomasina and I had some of it but there was far too much for us and so we fetched George and Marmalade who took it away with them. It was so heavy that they had to take it in turns to drag it off. George said that he thought it would last them for days.

What puzzles me is, why was the Upright who wears a Skirt so cross with me if she didn't want the chicken herself?

Sometimes Uprights are beyond comprehension.

October 9th

After stalking it for well over an hour I caught a sparrow today. I was very, very pleased with myself. I've never managed to catch a bird before. I was so delighted that I rushed back to the house with the sparrow still in my mouth. I wanted Thomasina and the Uprights to see what I'd caught.

Thomasina's response was deeply gratifying. I know that deep in her heart she must have been more than slightly jealous. She has always considered herself the best hunter. But she was decent enough to hide whatever feelings of envy she might have had. She was very complimentary and I was deeply touched by some of her comments.

However, the Uprights responded in a very strange way. The Upright who wears a Skirt was in the kitchen and when she saw me struggling to get in through the cat flap with the sparrow in my mouth she burst into tears.

I confess that at first I thought they were tears of pride. But it quickly became clear that she wasn't pleased with me at all. On the contrary, she was angry. At first she tried to get the sparrow away from me. And then she started waving the kitchen broom at me.

I ran out of the kitchen feeling quite confused. It quite spoilt the occasion for me.

Desperate for an explanation I left the bird lying on the lawn and set off to find George. I knew that he would have the answer. George understands Uprights far better than any cat I know.

112

"Uprights have a soft spot for birds," George told me. "Don't ask me to explain it because I can't. There isn't any logical explanation for it."

But they don't like mice or rats, do they?" I asked him.

George shook his head. "They hate them. And some Uprights are frightened of them."

"It doesn't seem logical to me," I said.

"You'll just have to learn to accept that Uprights often aren't logical," said George. "They adore hedgehogs and they quite like moles. But they have absolutely no real feelings for shrews and voles."

"Is it just sparrows that they like then?" I asked George.

He shook his head. "They like sparrows least of all," he told me. "Apart from starlings perhaps."

"So which birds do they like?"

"I believe that robins are their favourites," said George.

I asked him why Uprights like robins but he said he didn't know.

Finally, there was one other question that I had to ask. "What about squirrels?" I said. "Uprights like squirrels don't they?"

George nodded wisely. "They do."

"But they're only rats with bushy tails," I said. "And I thought Uprights hated rats."

George reached out patted the side of my head with his paw. "Uprights can be quite a puzzle," he said.

October 11th

Lapsong II arrived in the garden today with a huge rosette hanging around her neck. She looked very silly indeed.

"I won it at a cat show," she replied when Thomasina asked her where she'd got it.

She explained that every few months her Upright takes her to an arena where hundreds of cats are put on display.

"What for?" asked Thomasina innocently.

"To be judged, of course," answered Lapsong II.

Both Thomasina and I looked at her in astonishment. "What have they all done wrong?" I asked her.

"Lapsong II arrived with a huge rosette around her neck. She looked very silly."

Lapsong II threw back her head and sniffed disdainfully. "You really are very ignorant," she said. "It's not that sort of judging at all."

She explained that the idea is for Uprights who do the judging to wander around among the displayed cats and choose the best looking.

"But what's the point of it all?" I asked, genuinely confused.

"To win a cup and a rosette," explained Lapsong II.

"I think it's dreadfully degrading," said Thomasina.
"I think it's silly," I said.
"I think you're both just jealous," said Lapsong II.
But she was wrong. We weren't.

October 14th

Thomasina and I had to go to see the Upright who smells of Antiseptic to have our annual injections. I quite like him. He's firm but gentle and although I can't pretend that I like the injections he doesn't hurt me too much.

When I was a kitten I remember going to see an Upright who smells of Antiseptic who never explained anything. I don't know what he was like with other cats but he always treated me in a very cavalier manner. To be honest I always felt that I was just a piece of meat. Even when he did try to be friendly (usually only when one of my Uprights was around) I never got the impression that it was from the heart. He didn't really *care*.

"I remember losing the feeling in most of my body and then I remember everything going rather fuzzy."

In truth, I have to confess that my view of Uprights who smell of Antiseptic is slightly coloured by an experience I once had when I was a kitten. I was quite small at the time and I wasn't really aware of what was going on, but for some reason or other I had to have an operation. I remember having an injection. I remember losing the feeling in most of my body and then I remember everything going rather fuzzy. I could still see vague outlines and I could still hear. But it was a bit like looking and listening through a great, fluffy cotton wool cloud.

Then, and I can remember this as clearly as anything, I heard the Upright who smells of Antiseptic say: "Don't worry now young kitty. Everything is going to be all right."

I might have been sleepy and dozy at the time, but I knew very well that I wasn't Kitty. I was Alice. But there wasn't a thing I could do to warn the Upright who smells of Antiseptic that he was about to make a mistake and operate on the wrong cat. I couldn't move, I couldn't run away and I couldn't miaow. It was an awful experience which I relive in my nightmares.

As it happens, I suppose he must have found out that I wasn't Kitty before the operation was much older. I certainly don't think he did anything to me that he shouldn't have done!

October 16th

George was hanging around in the garden today looking very bedraggled and sorry for himself. It has been raining non stop for four days and nights and the cellar where he normally sleeps is flooded out. He told us that he hadn't eaten for a day and a half.

"Come back with us and have something to eat," said Thomasina. "Alice and I didn't finish our breakfast this morning. Come and help yourself."

George looked uncertain. He is probably the proudest cat I've ever met.

"You'd be doing us a favour," said Thomasina. "If you don't eat it then the Uprights will leave it there for hours. It'll go all crusty and horrid but they still won't give us anything fresh until it's gone."

Thomasina was exaggerating and I was about to intervene and contradict her. And then I realised that she was trying to make George feel better about accepting what he would see as charity.

"Please George," I said. "We'd be very grateful."

"George was hungry, damp and cold. He followed us back to the kitchen."

Normally I doubt if George would have been so easily persuaded. But he was hungry and damp and cold. And he followed us back to the house and into the kitchen.

Thomasina and I were watching him enjoy the remains of our breakfast when the Upright who wears a Skirt came into the kitchen. What ensued was the most embarrassing and humiliating moment of my life.

The Upright who wears a Skirt took one look at George with his head buried in our food bowl and leapt forwards angrily. I've never seen her looking so fearless. I found it difficult to believe that this was the same Upright who had shown herself to be terrified of mice, voles, shrews and all other small creatures.

It took George a moment or two to realise that something was wrong. And when he did finally see the Upright who wears a Skirt bearing down on him he was very startled. He bared his teeth and arched his back but he didn't stand a chance. The Upright who wears a Skirt had picked up the kitchen broom and within seconds George was being unceremoniously pushed out through the back door.

Thomasina and I just stared after him in disbelief. George was our friend. We had invited him into our home. And the Upright who wears a Skirt had ejected him.

The word "humiliating" doesn't even begin to describe the emotions we felt.

But to crown it all, as George scurried off down the garden, the Upright who wears a Skirt turned round to Thomasina and I and tried to stroke us both.

"Never mind," she said. "The nasty cat has gone now."

Thomasina and I just looked at her in dismay.

I don't think I'll ever really understand Uprights, however long I live.

October 18th

I spent this afternoon sitting on the bedroom window seat thinking of things to be grateful for.

Here is my list.

I am grateful that I am a cat and not an Upright. I know that Uprights are supposed to be cleverer than cats, but being an Upright seems often to be an unrewarding experience.

I am grateful that we do not live near to a road.

I am grateful that I have a funny white splodge under my chin. If it wasn't for that I might have been exhibited

at Shows. I can think of nothing more tedious than having to sit still all day while strangers stare.

I am grateful that I am not a mouse. If I were a mouse life would be miserable.

I am grateful that it is not Friday. On Fridays we usually have fish for supper and I hate fish.

I am grateful that I am not a dog. I would not like to be a dog.

I am grateful that I do not live with the Upright in Bickersleigh Gardens. She has 16 cats. I would not like to have to share a home with 16 other cats.

October 29th

I brought a mouse into the kitchen this evening and was so startled to find the Upright in Trousers helping with the washing up that I let it go. The Upright who wears a Skirt spends a lot of time in the ktichen, but the Upright in Trousers hardly ever enters that room.

Inevitably, the Upright who wears a Skirt squealed and screamed and tried to climb up onto the sink. The Upright in Trousers opened the back door and unceremoniously threw me outside.

The whole incident was over in twenty seconds.

Standing outside, I could hear the Upright in Trousers chasing the mouse round and round the kitchen.

And eventually I heard him swearing and poking about under the refrigerator with a long broom handle.

I can't imagine what made them think that they could catch the mouse without my help. They really are the worst hunters I've ever come across. I think it is nice that they should want to try. But they really do have to be prepared to spend a little time learning how to hunt before they try out their skills.

I have little doubt that there is now a third mouse living behind or underneath the refrigerator.

The Uprights so enjoyed the sport last night that I brought another mouse in while they were having tea. I know I complain about them occasionally but they're not all that bad and I think they deserve a treat from time to time. But somehow it didn't seem to go down quite so well. Perhaps they were only pretending to enjoy themselves yesterday so as not to hurt my feelings.

The Upright who wears a Skirt leapt up onto her chair and wrapped her skirt around her legs. The Upright in Trousers got so excited that he started throwing things. The table mat and the salt cellar only just missed me and a soup spoon brushed my back. If I hadn't known better I might have thought he was throwing them at me.

And then he picked me up and threw me out into the kitchen!

Yet another display of unacceptable bad manners. It was my mouse after all. One that I'd been keeping an eye on for three whole days. And a good runner too. I scratched and miaowed at the door to let them know that I thought they were behaving badly, but they didn't take any notice.

For about twenty minutes the Upright in Trousers chased the mouse round and round the dining room. Judging by the noise he made he must have knocked over just about everything in the room. When I'm chasing a mouse I take great care not to knock anything over. I always feel so guilty if I smash anything. But when they're hunting it's a different story, of course.

The end was predictable.

After creating havoc, The Upright in Trousers opened the kitchen door and let me in again. I pretended I didn't know what he wanted. I just sat there and looked up at him, holding my head ever so slightly on one side. Eventually after he'd stroked me and tickled me under the chin for two or three minutes I let him pick me up

"It was under the sideboard. I'd seen it hiding there the minute I'd entered the room."

and put me down where he thought he'd last seen the mouse.

It wasn't there, of course. It was hiding under the sideboard. I'd seen it the minute I entered the room.

He wouldn't believe me. I kept clawing at the sideboard and looking up at him and he kept picking me up and dumping me down by the fire tongs. Eventually the message got through and he gently lifted the sideboard at one corner.

I caught it easily.

The Upright who wears a Skirt screamed and pulled her skirt even tighter around her legs. The Upright in

Trousers clearly didn't know what to do. So I took the mouse outside and ate it behind the azaleas.

November 4th

Thomasina had a terrible accident this evening. She rushed in through the cat flap far too quickly and two of the longest whiskers on her left side snapped off.

It wasn't as if she'd been running away from danger. She had simply heard the Upright who wears a Skirt open the cupboard where our food is kept. And, as ever, she had wanted to get to the dish first. There is always plenty for both of us, but Thomasina always wants to be the first to get her head into the bowl.

I sometimes think that she must have had a very deprived kittenhood.

Anyway, she now has two whiskers missing on her left side. She still has enough whiskers there to help her decide whether gaps are too narrow for her to get through so there won't be any grave practical problems arising as a result of this accident. But it just doesn't look quite right and Thomasina, like most of us, is very particular about her appearance.

She asked me if they would ever grow back again.

I lied and told her that I thought they would eventually. But that it would take a long time.

I know it was probably wrong to lie to her but I feel that if she thinks they will grow back again then she will worry far less. And if she thinks it will take a long time then she won't be forever checking to see whether they have shown any improvement.

November 7th

For nearly a week I've had my eye on a field mouse that lives in the rockery. It's an odd place for a field

mouse to live but he seems happy enough there. Like many field mice he probably doesn't know that he is supposed to live in a field of swaying corn.

To be honest, I rather suspect that it is a field mouse that Thomasina caught once before. It walks with a slight limp and is probably the mouse that she caught before she was attacked by a hawk. Well, Thomasina says that she was attacked by a hawk. Personally, I rather suspect that the hawk saw the mouse and thought it might have a chance at an easy snack. Whatever the truth of the matter is, Thomasina panicked and dropped the mouse which, in all the confusion, dragged itself into the under- growth.

I've noticed that the mouse always emerges from his hideaway very cautiously. He pops his nose out first of all. Then, when he's convinced that he can't smell danger, he pops his head out. Then he looks from side to side, cautiously checking the immediate neighbourhood for any threats. Only when he is absolutely convinced that it is safe to come out does he emerge.

All this makes it very difficult to catch him. He is probably the most cautious and careful mouse I've ever come across. Catching him became quite a challenge for me.

But I had noticed that there was one weakness in all these preparations. The mouse couldn't see what was above him on the rockery. His exit and entrance hole was about half way up the rockery face and he had an excellent view of everything that was happening in the garden below him. And he could see what was happening to the right or left. But he couldn't tell what was right over his head.

And with the scent of the rockery plants making it unusually difficult for him to pick up the scent of a cat I thought that I might have a very good chance if I waited just above the entrance hole for him to emerge.

And it worked too.

He came out just as cautiously as ever. He sniffed and

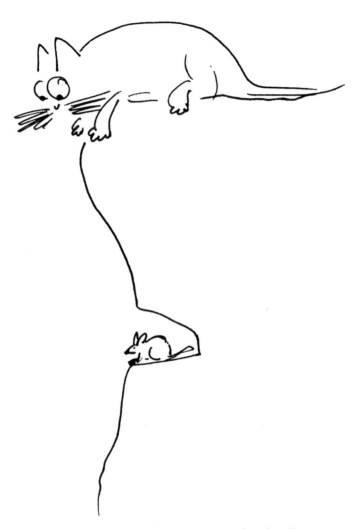

"The mouse couldn't see what was above him."

then he looked all around him. And only then did he
emerge from his hiding place.

Sometimes when you catch a mouse the skill all lies

in the actual pounce. You have to time things perfectly and move very quickly. This time the skill all lay in the planning and preparation. It was the easiest actual catch I've ever made.

As the mouse came out of his hole I just reached down with my paw and gave him a blow on the top of his head. For a moment or two I thought I'd killed him with my enthusiasm. But then I saw that I'd just stunned him.

Although all the action was over in a matter of seconds I had, in fact, been waiting for the mouse for the best part of three hours and I was cold and very wet by this time. It had rained twice while I'd been crouched in the rockery. Uprights sometimes don't realise how much effort goes into the catching of a mouse.

So I decided to take him indoors. I suspected that when he came round he'd provide some excellent killing practice.

The house was deserted so I took him straight through the kitchen and the living room and into the study. I used to enjoy killing practice in the kitchen but during the last month alone I've lost two mice under the refrigerator and I'm getting more than a little fed up of it. I can't get down the side of the refrigerator and I can't get my paw more than a couple of inches underneath it. Once a mouse has disappeared under there I don't have a chance of catching him again. (I wonder what ever happened to those two mice. Presumably they're still living under the refrigerator along with the one that the Uprights lost. If they start to breed Thomasina and I could have a source of endless indoor sport. That would be wonderful.)

The living room is quite good for killing practice, but I prefer the study. It's quieter at night and there aren't so many ornaments around. I tend to get rather excited when I'm chasing a mouse and the crash of a couple of ornaments soon brings the Uprights downstairs to see what is going on. I like to enjoy my killing practice without interruption.

I lay the mouse down on the rug underneath the desk and I waited to see what it would do. I waited and I waited and I waited. I even gave him a couple of slight taps on the side of the head just to remind him that he was supposed to be trying to escape. But he didn't move.

I had just decided that he must have been brain damaged by my initial blow when he made a move for it. He was fast. I have to admit that. I'd been waiting for so long that I was a bit off my guard and I missed him by inches. To be honest I'm not sure that I would have caught him even if I hadn't been off my guard. I've never seen a mouse move quite so quickly. And remember, this was a mouse with only three good legs.

While he'd been lying there on the rug he must have been planning his escape for he didn't falter for a second. He shot straight past me, underneath the arm chair and straight round the back of the night storage heater.

Within no more than five seconds of his first move he had completely disappeared again.

Of course, I waited to him to make another move, but it was like waiting for a butterfly to fly in a straight line. There wasn't a chance that he would come out. He was too clever. He was perfectly safe where he was and he knew it.

So in the end I gave up and went upstairs to sleep on the window seat. My main hope was that Thomasina would never find out what had happened.

November 8th

I was sitting in front of the fire today when a spark flew out and landed on my back. I now have a nasty singe mark there. When I told George about it he said that I should feign illness for a few days. He said that in most homes a singe mark is worth two jars of meat paste and a tin of condensed milk.

November 9th

I went downstairs this morning and popped into the study on the offchance that there might be some sign of the limping fieldmouse.

The Upright in Trousers almost trod on me as he marched out of the room clutching an old cardboard shoe box. I followed him into the kitchen and saw him go outside, still holding on to the box. As I sat on the doorstep I was horrified to see a twitching nose emerge as he lifted the top off the box. The limping fieldmouse!

I was rather proud of the fact that the Upright in Trousers had, at long last, managed to catch something. But he clearly needs more lessons.

November 17th

Ishmael is quite a good friend of ours. She lives about a mile and a half away in a small cottage down near the river. She is a thoughtful and kind cat and both Thomasina and I are very fond of her. But today we had a tremendous argument with her and I fear that it will be some time before we are invited to her cottage again. Ishmael takes herself very seriously and doesn't forgive and forget very easily.

Our argument started when Ismael said that she was going to spend the night out hunting rabbits. She said that she knew where the local rabbits played and that she was certain that she could catch one.

Thomasina and I immediately told her that we thought she was being silly.

"All night hunting is for tom cats," said Thomasina. "Alice and I both like late evening hunting, but we always make sure we don't stray too far from home. And we're always back in the house soon after midnight."

Ishmael scoffed at this. "I've never heard such

rubbish," she said crossly. "We can do anything that toms can do. We're just as good as they are."

"But rabbits . . . " said Thomasina . "I wouldn't like to try and catch a rabbit."

I told Ishmael that I didn't dispute that queens were just as good as toms. "It's just that our skills and strengths are different," I said.

But Ishmael said that I was betraying my sex and that she didn't want to listen any more. And with that she left us.

I thought about it quite a lot after she'd gone. I can understand the way she feels, of course. It is the fashion these days to try and pretend that there are no differences between the sexes. But it's all wrong. Pretending that there are no fundamental differences between a tom and a queen is as silly as pretending that there is no difference between day and night, between hot and cold or between wet and dry.

I've heard it claimed that the differences between toms and queens are fairly minor physical ones. Well, even though I would dispute the word "minor" I would still happily accept that toms and queens could reverse roles if the differences were purely physical.

But they aren't.

I think that there are other, very important differences between the sexes.

By and large queens have soft, protective, maternal instincts. Toms have more powerful, aggressive instincts. A queen's hormones prepare her for motherhood, feeding and home building. A tom's hormones prepare him for hunting and exploring.

Just imagine for a moment that there is a kitten lying in a corner miaowing its head off. And a perfectly normal, healthy pair of cats walk past. A tom and a queen. Now just stop and ask yourself how they will react.

The queen will stop, make comforting noises, lick the kitten, pick it up and take it somewhere soft and comfortable. The tom will look bewildered and rather worried.

128

He would clearly rather be somewhere else and he'll wander off as quickly as he can. A tom wouldn't dream of stopping to comfort a kitten.

Why do male and female cats respond in these different ways? Because of basic genetic and hormonal differences, that's why.

Cats like Ishmael find it easy to pretend that these differences don't exist. And, like Ishmael, they accuse anyone who disagrees with them of being ''sexist''.

Well, I think they're being silly. I would heartily disapprove if I thought that queens were regarded any less highly than toms. But I don't really think that happens at all. It infuriates me when I hear cats like Ishmael claiming that queens should be allowed to do all the things that toms can do, and that the differences between the sexes can be eradicated.

I pray that those differences will always exist.

Toms are better at some things than queens. And queens are better at some things than toms.

I, for one, like things the way they are.

November 23rd

I saw a frog today. I probably could have caught it if I'd really wanted to. But it kept hopping away out of reach.

November 25th

The Uprights came by this evening just as I was dragging a large meat bone out of the dustbin. They both seemed surprised, even startled, and stopped to watch me for

"I saw a frog today. I probably could have caught it. But it kept hopping away out of reach."

a while. At first I thought they were going to take the bone away from me. But they changed their minds.

"When I offered her that this afternoon she turned it down," I heard the Upright who wears a Skirt say as they walked away. "Sometimes I don't think I'll ever understand that cat."

If I hadn't been enjoying the bone so much I'd have run after her and tried to make her understand. She was absolutely right of course. She *had* offered me the bone that afternoon. And I *had* turned it down. I hadn't been the slightest bit hungry then. But this evening as I passed the bin I'd been feeling slightly peckish so I'd looked

"I don't think there is anything quite so tasty as something that has been lying in a dustbin for a few hours."

in, spotted the bone and taken a fancy to it straight away. There really was quite a lot of good, fresh meat still on it.

The impression I got from the Upright who wears a Skirt was that she was surprised that I would deign to eat something that had been in the dustbin at all.

And that I really don't understand.

Surely even the Uprights must realise that the circumstances and surroundings in which food is presented plays an important part in its attractiveness. Personally, I don't think there is anything quite so tasty as something that has been lying in a dustbin for a few hours. There are always so many other added flavours and tastes coming through.

And even Uprights do similar things. I've seen the Upright who wears a Skirt pick food off a plate that has been ready to go into the washing up bowl. And I've seen both of them eating fish and chips out of old newspaper. Where's the logic in that? They have cupboards full of expensive china and cutlery and yet they still eat with their fingers out of old newspapers.

The thing that really puzzles me about Uprights is their inconsistency.

December 1st

Thomasina mentioned today that it is some time since we saw George. I hope that he is well.

December 6th

The Uprights have noticed that I haven't taken them any more mice to play with. And they're trying to get round me. Today both of them made quite a fuss of me. The Upright bought me some fresh liver from the butchers.

But I'm not going to be "bought" with a plateful of fresh liver (which I can't help saying wasn't all that fresh and, if the truth be known, had probably been sold off cheap). I'll make them wait a few days yet before I bring them another mouse of mine to play with.

December 9th

After weeks of trying I caught a bat today. But once I'd caught it I wasn't sure what to do with it. I had to kill it quickly to stop it flying away again. I tried biting through its skin but an old shoe would have been more palatable. I don't think I'll bother catching any more.

December 12th

I spent three hours hunting a vole this afternoon. As soon as I had caught it the rain started. Since I do not like getting wet for no good reason I took the vole into the kitchen for a little indoor sport. The vole, however, was not prepared to behave in a very sporting way. Within moments of my letting it go it had scurried underneath the cooker. Since I can't get underneath the cooker and the vole didn't dare come out we had to be satisfied with a stalemate.

"I left the vole where it was and went to sleep on a pile of clean washing."

So I left the vole where it was and went to sleep on top of a pile of clean washing. I knew that I would hear if the vole tried to escape. I am a light sleeper.

Of all small creatures I think I like voles least of all. They have a strange, unpleasant peculiarly bitter taste.

December 15th

We went in search of George today. But couldn't find him anywhere. Penelope says that if she sees Oscar she will ask him if he knows anything about George.

December 18th

Thomasina and I had a terrible shock this morning.

Thomasina was the first to make the discovery. She had her breakfast and then sleepily pushed her way through the cat flap.

She was back in the kitchen within seconds.

"Raining?" I asked her. I know how much she hates the rain.

She shook her head.

"What is it then?" I asked puzzled, "A dog?"

Another shake of the head.

She was clearly too startled to say anything so I cautiously pushed my head through the cat flap, keeping all four paws firmly rooted on the kitchen floor.

I could hardly believe what I saw.

The whole garden had turned white.

I turned back and looked at Thomasina. She was examining her paws. They too were covered in white. But even as we stared at them the white substance seemed to disappear. Very cautiously she touched her left forepaw with her tongue.

"What does it taste like?" I whispered.

Thomasina paused for a moment and then licked at her paw again. "Water," she replied after a moments thought. "It tastes just like water."

By now the white that had been on her paws had all vanished.

Slowly I opened the cat flap again. But this time as well as poking my head out I tentatively put my right front paw outside on the step. The white stuff felt cold but not unpleasant. It was soft and yet rather crunchy.

Bravely I pushed through the flap and stepped outside completely. I could hear Thomasina coming through the flap behind me. As we walked around we lifted our paws up into the air and shook them free of the white stuff before we took another step. It was a most peculiar experience. And then I suddenly realised that the white stuff was getting deeper and deeper. Instead of just covering my paws it was so deep that I was sinking in right up to my body. I didn't like it at all. And to be perfectly honest I began to panic a little. I backed out as fast as I possibly could and, followed by Thomasina, made a rush back for the cat flap.

By the time we got back into the kitchen we were both shivering with excitement, cold and, I confess, fear.

We decided to spend the rest of the day indoors.

December 19th

I woke up this morning dreaming that a rough barked tree was rubbing itself against my head. I quickly discovered that Thomasina was licking my face.

"It's gone," she whispered.

"What's gone," I asked her. I didn't have the faintest idea what she was talking about.

"The white stuff," she answered. "I've had a look outside."

Suddenly I remembered what she was talking about. I stood up, stretched and padded downstairs behind her.

She was absolutely right, too. The white stuff had completely disappeared. The whole garden was very wet and it had clearly rained during the night and washed it all away.

I don't suppose we will ever know just what it was. I bet it gave the Uprights quite a surprise too.

December 23rd

I killed an enormous shrew last night and deposited it in the kitchen so that the Uprights could see it. I thought they'd be pleased. I even thought they might be tempted to taste it. I don't like shrew. I think they taste horrid. But an Upright might like the taste. Or so I thought.

But when the Upright in Trousers came into the kitchen and saw the shrew he obviously didn't want it. He opened the back door, picked up the shrew by its tail and hurled it as far as he could.

And then he looked at me.

I think he wanted me to run and get it so that he could throw it again. I've seen Uprights doing that with dogs in the park.

Well, I'm not a dog and I'm not that stupid. I had no intention of playing his silly game.

But I did think I'd have a little fun with him. I ran off in the direction the shrew had taken and then hid among the bushes. A good ten minutes afterwards I could see the Upright still standing in the doorway waiting to see if I would take the shrew back to him.

December 25th

I got up this morning and was presented by the Uprights with a small packet wrapped in brightly coloured paper.

I looked across the room and saw that Thomasina, who'd got up a few moments before me, had also received a gift of similar shape and size. Neither of us knew what to do. I sniffed at mine but it didn't really smell of anything. Thomasina patted hers with a paw but although the paper rustled it didn't move.

"I was presented by the Uprights with a small packet wrapped in brightly coloured paper."

With obvious excitement our two Uprights picked up the packets and unwrapped them. The Upright in Trousers unwrapped mine and the Upright who wears a Skirt unwrapped Thomasina's.

We had both been given rubber mice.

It was one of those occasions when I was glad that the Uprights don't speak our language. At least I didn't have to try and think of something to say. I looked across at Thomasina. She looked equally puzzled.

Desperate to assure the Uprights that their gift was received in the right spirit I reached forward and gave the rubber mouse a pat. It fell over sideways. I gave it another pat and it moved another inch or two. Thomasina just watched. And then I gave it a harder tap. This time it made a strange sound. A bit like a door that needed oiling.

I don't pretend to understand why, but it seems that the Uprights have bought us both rubber mice that need oiling.

December 28th

Dreadful, dreadful news.

George is dead.

He was run over by a motor car over a fortnight ago. According to Oscar he managed to crawl into the gutter and died there quite alone. What a dreadful way to go. Poor George. It really is about time something was done about the way that motor cars race around on the roads. George is by no means the first cat to die this way. And I very much doubt if he will be the last.

George was one of the kindest, most thoughtful and most intelligent cats I have ever met. He was generous, wise, compassionate and never slow to help a stranger.

I was always honoured to count George among my

friends. He taught me a great deal. And he was always patient with Thomasina and myself.

We will miss him terribly.

What a sad end to the year.

I don't know what else to write.

December 30th

I sincerely hope that no one ever reads this diary. But since I am writing my memoirs I have to be honest.

Last night I caught a shrew which I thought I would take into the house for a little pleasant hunting practice. It seemed a game, sporty sort of shrew. I thought it would help take my mind off George's tragic death.

I don't think I have ever underestimated a creature more than I underestimated that shrew.

I took it into the hall because although there are plenty of hiding places there, none of them are completely out of reach. And then I dropped the shrew right in the middle of the floor and lay down to wait and see what it did next.

To my astonishment it didn't run away, as I'd expected it to do, but just sat there up on its hind legs and made the most extraordinary noise. I could hardly believe that such a small shrew was making such a lot of noise.

Naturally, I moved closer to quieten it down. It was making enough noise to wake up the Uprights and I'd had enough of their hunting attempts for the time being.

I thought that a gentle tap on the head would persuade it to keep quiet and run and hide.

That was when I got my second surprise.

Instead of running away, the shrew leapt up at my face and bit me on the nose.

I feel almost too embarrassed to write this down. How could I ever hold my head up again if anyone knew that I'd been bitten on the nose by a shrew! Thomasina would

"The shrew bit me on the nose!"

never let me forget it. Even dear old Penelope would be shocked.

But my shame doesn't stop there. I was so startled by this that instead of reaching forward and killing the shrew instantly I backed away a little. It was a reflex move.

And while I was smarting and rubbing my bleeding nose the shrew disappeared.

When I realised what had happened I spent ages looking for it. But I couldn't find it anywhere. There is a tiny gap at the side of the front door and I can only conclude that it somehow managed to squeeze through there and get outside.

So there it is. My most shameful night. If anyone ever reads this I shall deny that it ever happened and claim that I was practising my skills as a storyteller.

December 31st

So, another year has gone. It seems only yesterday that I started keeping this diary. There have been a lot of happy days and some very sad days. At least I will have my diary to remind me of it all.

I wonder what next year will bring?

I already have my new diary ready. It is in front of me as I write. At the moment it is nothing but a year of blank pages.

I look forward to filling them.

142

Alice's Adventures

After the publication of her first book Alice was inundated with fan mail and requests urging her to put pen to paper once more. The result is this, her second volume of memoirs.

In her second book she records yet more adventures and mishaps with many a tear being shed during this eventful year. Full of the illustrations and humour so much-loved by readers of her first book.

"I didn't think Alice could surpass her first book – but she has. I really loved *Alice's Adventures*. The saddest moment came when I finished it. When will the next volume be ready?"
(Mrs K., Somerset)

"We have had cats for over 30 years and Alice describes incidents which are so real that we nearly died laughing at them." *(Mrs O., Leeds)*

"*Alice's Adventures* is the loveliest book I have ever read. It captures everything brilliantly. Thinking back over the book I can't help smiling. I have never enjoyed a book as much." *(Mrs H., Edinburgh)*

Price £9.99 (hardback)

Alice and Other Friends

Thousands of readers have already discovered the joys of *Alice's Diary* and *Alice's Adventures* which have sold tens of thousands of copies and entranced animal lovers all over the world.

Vernon Coleman 'helped' Alice to write and illustrate these two books. Now, at last, here is Vernon Coleman's own account of life with Alice and her half sister Thomasina.

Charming, touching and intensely personal, this book is packed with stories, anecdotes and reminiscences about Alice and the many other creatures Vernon Coleman has met, known and lived with. There are, of course, many stories about Vernon Coleman's four pet sheep. The book is liberally and beautifully illustrated with numerous line drawings by the author.

Price 12.99 (hardback)

Other cat books by Vernon Coleman include

We Love Cats

We Love Cats is a real celebration of cats and is packed with humour and insight into the way cats think, behave and quietly run our lives. We Love Cats contains over 100 new and original Vernon Coleman drawings (he calls them catoons) plus poems, limericks and amazing facts about cats.

Price £12.99 (hardback)

Cats' Own Annual

A chance to see the world through the eyes of some very literate cats. Packed with lists, poems, limericks and drawings. Contains cats' answers to the questions all Uprights ask.

Price £12.99 (hardback)

The Secret Lives of Cats

The first time Uprights have ever been allowed access to the private correspondence exchanged by cats. The Secret Lives of Cats is full of wisdom and humour and will make you smile, cry and, at the end, feel warm all over. Illustrated by the author.

Price £12.99 (hardback)

The Cat Basket

Another collection of fascinating facts and entertaining anecdotes. Twenty two chapters comprehensively illustrated with Vernon 'catoons'. Another must for cat lovers everywhere.

Price £12.99 (hardback)

Cat Fables

We can learn a great deal from cats. Not just about their behaviour; we can also learn lessons that apply to us, too. Watch and listen to cats and we can learn an enormous amount that will help us through life.

How true are the stories in this book? Well, that's for you to decide. But each story has been chosen because it contains a message; a 'moral' if you like, that can perhaps also help us in the way we live our day-to-day lives.

Beautifully illustrated throughout.

Price £12.99 (hardback)

The Bilbury Chronicles

A young doctor arrives to begin work in the small village of Bilbury. This picturesque hamlet is home to some memorable characters who have many a tale to tell, and Vernon Coleman weaves together a superb story full of humour and anecdotes. The Bilbury books will transport you back to the days of old-fashioned, traditional village life where you never needed to lock your door, and when a helping hand was only ever a moment away. The first novel in the series.

"I am just putting pen to paper to say how very much I enjoyed *The Bilbury Chronicles*. I just can't wait to read the others." *(Mrs K., Cambs)*

"...a real delight from cover to cover. As the first in a series it holds out the promise of entertaining things to come" *(Daily Examiner)*

"The Bilbury novels are just what I've been looking for. They are a pleasure to read over and over again." *(Mrs C., Lancs)*

Price £12.99 (hardback)

The Man Who Inherited a Golf Course

Trevor Dunkinfield, the hero of this novel, wakes up one morning to discover that he is the owner of his very own golf club – fairways, bunkers, clubhouse and all. This unexpected present lands in Trevor's lap as a result of a distant uncle's will which he discovers, to his dismay, contains several surprising clauses. To keep the club he must win an important match – and he's never played a round of golf in his life!

"This scenario is tailor made for Vernon Coleman's light and amusing anecdotes about country life and pursuits. His fans will lap it up." *(Sunday Independent)*

"Hugely enjoyable, in the best tradition of British comic writing." *(Evening Chronicle)*

"Light-hearted entertainment ... very readable." *(Golf World)*

Price £12.99 (hardback)

The Village Cricket Tour

Traditional village cricket has a special place in the hearts of all true cricket lovers. Freshly mown grass. The smell of linseed oil. Cucumber sandwiches and sponge cake.

Once in a lifetime a book is written which truly captures not only the soul and spirit of the game but also the essential, though often accidental, comedy of amateur village cricket.

Vernon Coleman's novel is just such a book. It tells the story of a team of amateur cricketers who spend two weeks of their summer holidays on tour in the West Country. It proves to be a most eventful fortnight full of mishaps and adventures as the team play their way around the coastline of Devon and Cornwall.

"I enjoyed it immensely. He has written a book that will entertain, amuse and warm the cockles of tired old hearts."
(*Peter Tinniswood, Punch*)

"It is the funniest book about cricket that I have ever read. In fact it is the funniest book I have read since Three Men in a Boat."
(*Chronicle & Echo*)

"His powers of observation combine with his penchant for brilliant word pictures to create a most delightful book that will appeal to all those who appreciate humour and sharp characterisation."
(*The Sunday Independent*)

Price £12.99 (hardback)

*For a catalogue of Vernon Coleman's books
please write to:*

Publishing House, Trinity Place, Barnstaple,
Devon EX32 9HG, England

| Telephone | 01271 328892 |
| Fax | 01271 328768 |

Outside the UK:
| Telephone | +44 1271 328892 |
| Fax | +44 1271 328768 |

Or visit our website: www.vernoncoleman.com